PURRDER, SHE WROTE

THE DETECTIVE WHISKERS COZY MYSTERY SERIES

BOOK FOUR

CHRIS ABERNATHY

Purrder, She Wrote

A Detective Whiskers Cozy Mystery

ONE

"After I killed him, I encased his body in bronze and displayed it as a statue outside his favorite football team's stadium."

The young man speaking in the crowded lobby of the Parrot Eyes Inn wore a self-congratulatory smile to match his flashy clothes and seemed briefly lost in his imagination.

His audience was an attractive young woman and a senior gentleman wearing an old fishing hat like the one made famous by Ernest Hemingway. They laughed, drawing looks from a few individuals pulling suitcases. Paradise Cove hadn't had this many visitors since the summer beach season ended several weeks before.

"And you, Isabella?"

The man who had made the confession clasped his hands to his chest and waited eagerly for an answer.

"My first?"

"Yes."

"I pushed him off the roof of an abandoned warehouse then put a parachute on his body and rolled it out of an airplane over Yellowstone. Some hikers saw the body fall so it was discovered quickly, but by the time they realized he had died elsewhere, the crime scene was cleaned up."

The gentleman in the hat let out an appreciative "oooooh" as the younger man typed a note into his phone.

Isabella pointed a finger at the phone. "Don't copycat me, Max, or you'll be my next!"

My fur bristled at the term "copycat." As if cats were prone to copying what humans do. Ridiculous. Most of us couldn't care less what humans do other than feed us and clean our litter boxes unless it's our job to care. Which in my case, it is. I'm a detective. Detective Whiskers.

The inaccurate and inconsiderate word, of course, wasn't my main concern. First and foremost was the casual discussion of killing people.

As a cat, I was used to hearing humans confess things that they wouldn't normally say in front of strangers. It was one of my greatest advantages as a detective, along with my feline sense of smell and being so close to clues on the ground. Clues that taller detectives often overlooked. But I had never overheard such casual talk about murders. If I had the ability to talk to humans, I would have made a quick exit and returned with Chief Anderson. Instead, I turned away to hide the police badge dangling from my collar. A floor-to-ceiling mirror allowed me to watch from behind a plastic palm tree as the older man glanced around conspiratorially. He spoke in a soft voice with a distinguished English accent.

"My first victim ... "

Isabella interrupted. "Was shot with a poison dart from a Mardi Gras float in New Orleans. I remember that one!"

The man shook his head. "That's what everybody *thinks* but it wasn't my first." He leaned in and softened his voice even more, pulling his hat an inch lower and squinting his eyes. "The poor man was killed at high noon in a gun duel against an alien pretending to be a cowboy."

Max stepped backward and stared. The woman grimaced.

"And now you know why I changed my name to Victor Bloodworth - so no one unfortunate enough to read that book would know that I wrote it!"

Victor tipped his hat and made his exit, walking into the hallway past a sign that read "Welcome Murder Mystery Writers." He turned back to his laughing audience and added, "Should you ever stumble upon one of the very few copies in existence, I'll gladly pay you £50,000 and open my oldest bottle of Scotch while we burn it!"

The black and white fur on my back, which had been standing straight up, fell back into place. I breathed out a long sigh. For one of very few times in my life, I appreciated my inability to speak to humans. And I was extremely grateful that Kojak, my K-9 officer friend, wasn't nearby. He would have never stopped teasing me. I shamefully walked away from the mirror so that I could no longer see my badge reflecting at me and zigzagged my way between legs to check on my human, Sheila Mason, who was standing behind the long, wooden reception desk.

Evelyn, the elderly owner of the Inn, came out of her office holding a screwdriver. "I'll be right back, Sheila. Thanks again for getting everybody checked in. You're the best friend in the whole world!" She rushed toward the elevator where a man was growing agitated as he repeatedly pressed the UP button. "Kevin! Put those bags down and help me get the elevator working again."

I had to dodge quickly as a familiar figure placed a set of luggage where I had been standing by the desk. A few guests had gathered behind the button-pusher. They looked at each other warily and walked to the stairwell. One man in an obnoxiously bright Hawaiian shirt spoke loudly. "You won't catch me getting on that thing!"

"That's a relief," a man still waiting at the elevator joked, drawing laughter from most of the group.

As Kevin reached the elevator I spotted a bulge at the bottom of his pants leg near his left ankle — low and hardly noticeable for people, but right at eye level for a cat. It surprised me that Evelyn had agreed to let him stay with her during his house arrest. Having him interact with guests may have been an even bigger mistake. Even if he behaved perfectly, at least one observant human was bound to see what I had seen and the gossip would start.

"Isabella Nightshade! You've got some nerve showing up here."

In the center of the lobby, a conservatively dressed woman held her nose high in the air and averted her gaze as she passed Isabella and Max. Max called out in defense of his companion.

"You're just jealous, Buffy! Maybe one day your rich daddy will buy you a best-seller."

Isabella, smiling and relaxed moments ago, had begun shaking. She covered her face with her hands.

"Hey, don't let them get to you," Max told her. "Winning is winning. I don't even care if the rumors are true. You hit #1 on the Times, and that advance you got paid for your next book? Boom! You can laugh all the way to the bank."

Isabella pulled mascara-covered hands away from her face and glared at Max.

"C'mon," he continued. "You're making the most of your new fame and fortune, aren't you? From what I see, you've hired a personal trainer. That tight skirt is looking good on you. It would look even better on my ... "

The whole lobby heard Isabella's hand slap against Max's cheek. Most gawked as she walked off in a huff. Max stared at her skirt and smirked.

Victor Bloodworth, oblivious to the drama or refusing to acknowledge it, passed Isabella heading in the opposite direction. He had re-entered the lobby and walked purposefully to the reception desk where Sheila was helping someone check in.

Victor moved beside the other guest, tipping his hat, and interrupted as politely as possible. "Excuse me. Might I have a word?"

Apologizing to the woman checking in, Sheila allowed Victor to lead her down the desk to a quiet corner.

I was curious so I padded across the stained and worn carpet floor. I know. Curiosity killed the cat. But you can't exactly be a world-class detective without it, can you?

"I don't want to cause this hotel any more problems than it already has, but an extremely important item has gone missing and I need it back. Urgently."

"But you just checked in. Are you sure it's at the Inn?"

Victor took a deep breath before replying slowly to make himself very clear. "I am not one to throw out idle accusations. My bags were taken to my room and when I opened them, a vital item was missing. If it is not returned to me by 10:00 PM then I will be forced to go to the police which, I suspect, will put an end to the limited freedom being enjoyed by the man wearing an ankle monitor. Yes, I noticed it when he walked away with my bags. Please don't make me regret my hasty decision to avoid causing a scene. The proprietor of this once beautiful Inn seems like a lovely woman. She also bears a strong resemblance to the man in question. While it is honorable that she is giving her son a second chance, let us hope that he, also, can find some honor within himself before it is too late. Now, if you'll excuse me, I need to return to my room."

With that, Victor smiled and tipped his hat again to the waiting guest as he walked slowly back toward the hallway.

As a detective, I was impressed by his observational skills and powers of deduction. It made me want to read his books. Preferably on an electronic device. Turning pages with furry paws isn't easy and Sheila gets upset when I use my claws to punch holes in the paper. But we cats are a skeptical bunch and I did not share Victor's optimism that Kevin might discover some personal code of honor. He had passed up too many opportunities before.

Sheila, her face drained of color, glanced at Evelyn and Kevin as she rushed back behind the reception desk and apologized again to the waiting guest.

Two

Sheila was ready for a quiet nap on a beach chair when we got home to Sunset Cottage, our perfect little house overlooking the beach with a short boardwalk leading to the sand and water. When she had filled in for Evelyn at the reception desk previously, it had been easy and boring. Not this time.

"You're lucky, Whiskers. You can stay home and take naps for the rest of the day. I've got to be back to help at the bar in a couple of hours."

A catnap sounded good and I settled into my special cushion on the living room bookshelf. Sheila's crafty friend Julia had made it for me using Fred's old uniform and I took the best naps on it. When I poked and prodded at the fabric it still released just a little of his scent. Fred, my former partner and mentor, was Sheila's husband for forty years. He was supposed to be with us here in Paradise Cove but, that's how life goes. You never know how much you have left so Sheila and I were trying to make the most of ours. I figured I probably had at least six of my nine lives left.

Everything Fred had taught me had come in handy in this town that had never seen a murder before we arrived earlier this year. That statistic changed quickly and I'd already solved three, with some help from Sheila and her new friends — the Paradise Cove Murder Society. They bonded quickly after Sheila was accused of stabbing our neighbor, Mitch. Mostly they sat on the deck drinking margaritas and laughing, which was what Tarrie Ann had planned when she showed up unexpectedly with an almost full pitcher and an almost empty glass.

"You can't expect us to sit at home crocheting after you've just met a bunch of the world's best murder mystery writers! We want the scoop!"

Sheila wagged her finger. "You've never crocheted in your life, Tarrie Ann."

"Busted. But I still want to hear all about it. Julia and Becky will be here soon."

A click-click-clicking noise from the front porch told me that Becky had already arrived. If Paradise Cove had a dress code it would be more likely to include Tarrie Ann's flip-flops and summer dress than Becky's stiletto heels and skirt suit but for Becky casual dress meant unbuttoning the vest on her suit. She made sure her real estate clients knew that she was serious about helping them buy their slice of paradise.

Becky walked in without knocking, her phone at her ear.

"I'll let you know the minute I hear back from the seller."

"You'll put that phone down and pour yourself a margarita is what you'll do. Sheila's got to be back at the Inn soon, so no interruptions for unimportant things like work!"

There was a knock on the French doors leading out to the deck and the beach. Julia, wearing a modest one-piece swimsuit and a coverup, waved through the plantation shutters. She was holding a bag of chips and a bowl.

Tarrie Ann picked up the pitcher and the last empty glass, expertly juggling it along with her own refilled glass. "I hereby call this meeting of the Paradise Cove Murder Society to order!"

The party was heading outside. I knew from experience that there would be too much laughing for me to enjoy my nap so I hopped down from the shelf and slid through the door with them. I always prefer the real door to the little pet door that closes on my tail if I don't rush through. It's very undignified.

"Your students won't die if they see you in a two-piece," Tarrie Ann teased Julia. "You've still got the body for it. Rock it!"

Julia pulled her cover-up tighter and sat down at the table.

Tarrie Ann dipped a chip into Julia's bowl and took a bite. "Wow! Your guacamole is always amazing. I'd ask you for the recipe but I'd rather you just keep making it for us!"

Becky sat down in a chaise lounge and threw out the first question for Sheila. "I want to hear about Victor Bloodworth. Did you meet him?"

"Twice."

"I knew it! He already hit on you, didn't he?"

"More like threatened me, in the most courteous way possible."

Three margarita glasses were set down almost simultaneously as the light girl talk got serious.

"He thinks Kevin stole something from him. Which is probably true."

"Why did Evelyn let him move back in?" Julia asked. "He lied to her, tried to take over her business, and partnered up with that murderer Roger. They tried to frame you, Sheila! And you still help her at the Inn while he's living there?"

"Living *and* working." Sheila sighed. "She's got him carrying luggage and cleaning rooms. I guess she feels like she doesn't have a choice, at least until the trial. Even after agreeing to join us in testifying against Roger, they wouldn't let him out of prison without somebody taking responsibility for him. She's the only family he has. And, besides, she's barely able to keep the Inn open. Without him and me there's no way she could handle this conference and she needs the money to do some of the most urgent repairs. Becky, what did she say about the possible buyer you met?"

"She said she'd think about it, but I got the impression she wasn't serious. I told her not to think too long because if one more thing falls apart she may not be able to sell it."

Tarrie Ann took another sip of margarita. "If the Parrot Eyes Inn closes there won't be anywhere in town to buy a drink."

"Or anywhere for tourists to stay," Julia added. "And that would be the end for Sea Brews coffee, Sandy Scoops ice cream, pretty much all the businesses in town. They all lose money when the tourists are gone. The Home Owners Association would have to consider allowing vacation rental houses."

Becky shushed Julia. "Nosy Nancy would have a heart attack if she heard you say that ... which she probably did! She's tightened up all the loopholes in the HOA bylaws."

Sheila waved her arms. "Ok, ok. Enough doom and gloom. I've only got two hours before I go back to work and you all came over to hear about famous writers. I'll tell you this much, they don't seem to like each other very much!"

Gossip isn't my thing and I had been there with Sheila so I already knew what she was about to tell her friends and I decided it would be a good time to check in on some of my friends. I padded halfway down the boardwalk and then hopped into the sand, ignoring the rules about not walking in the dunes. I don't normally ignore rules, being a respectable detective, but some rules were only for humans. Cats like myself could make our way through the dunes without messing them up.

My friend Zappa *lived* in the dunes. Zappa was a calico and a male so if you know anything about cats you already know he's not normal. Maybe that's why I liked him. His hippie-dippy ways helped me relax, or 'chill' as he would say. And he liked me because I sometimes shared the catnip that Sheila gave me.

I tiptoed through the sand, careful not to disturb the ghost crab holes. Winding my way around the sea oats, I headed to the spot where I expected to find Zappa lying on his back enjoying the cool breeze coming in off the water. He wasn't there.

Stepping out to the edge of the dunes I could see Jimmy fishing from the pier. That explained Zappa's absence. He was waiting for a small fish to be tossed his way. I walked just a few feet down the edge of the dunes until I heard him speak.

"Hey, man. Just about supper time. You gonna join me for a bite?"

"Thanks, but Sheila already fed me. How's Jimmy doing today?"

"Couple of nibbles, man. No catches yet but I ain't worried. Your Sheila not gonna join him today?"

"Not today. I'm not sure she truly enjoys fishing. It was nice of him to teach her how, though. She likes sitting out there on the pier with him. But she's busy today. Big conference at the Inn. A bunch of mystery writers."

"That's cool."

We sat together, feeling the cool breeze and the warm sunshine while the lapping of the waves made my eyelids heavy. Before long I dozed off. Zappa kept one eye open and focused on Jimmy, waiting for a free meal. He wasn't the only one.

Blue, a great blue heron that lived nearby, was at the edge of the water a few feet down from the pier. Jimmy always gave Blue his first fish. She was a quiet one who didn't like to chat too much and

I'd learned it was best not to disturb her when she was waiting for a fish.

A barking noise from the pier woke me up. Jimmy had something on the line and Buster, his excitable dog, was encouraging him as he reeled it in. Blue inched closer to the pier, positioning herself close enough for Jimmy to toss her the fish but far enough away that Buster couldn't run over and play before she had a chance to spread her majestic wings.

I looked back to Sunset Cottage and saw golf carts leaving. The "meeting" had adjourned and Sheila would soon be headed back to the Inn. Maybe I should join her, I thought. Victor Bloodworth had shown some real skill with his observations and deductions. Perhaps there was something at this conference for a detective to learn.

I said goodbye to Zappa and padded back through the dunes.

THREE

The wall behind Sheila had three long shelves to display bottles. She couldn't reach the top shelf but it wouldn't be a problem because there weren't enough bottles to fill the lower two. Evelyn had stopped restocking all but the most popular drinks.

The bright lights exposed all the faults of the aging room. Coasters had been placed under several table legs to keep them from wobbling. Dust had settled along the tops of the miniature walls separating the booths. Threads of carpet rose up along a line crossing the room, unraveling where two pieces had been joined many years ago.

I sat on my favorite stool at the end of the bar by the wall. It was the best spot to see most of the room and hear the conversation at the bar. That's where people sat if they wanted to interact with strangers. I wasn't interested in eavesdropping on private conversations at the tables. Well, maybe I was curious but I had some manners.

The door creaked open halfway.

"Fifteen minutes," Sheila announced sharply while wiping down the bar top.

"It's Kevin. Mind if I come in?"

Sheila set down her rag and rubbed the back of her neck.

"C'mon in."

The door opened further and Kevin stepped inside tentatively. He stopped and looked at Sheila before walking up to the stool closest to the door.

"Something to drink?"

"Uh, no. Thanks. I, uh ... "

"I gotta open those doors in 15 ... 14 minutes, Kevin and this bar is not even clean, let alone set up properly. Spit it out."

Kevin sat silently, looking down.

"Maybe this will help." Sheila grabbed a glass and poured three fingers of whisky then got back to work with her rag.

"Sorry. I, uh, just wanted to tell you I'm sorry."

"For ... ?"

"I never thought Roger would kill anybody. He said we could build a new hotel and make a fortune if y'all sold us your houses and I saw this place falling apart. I wanted to help Mom ... "

Sheila threw the rag down.

"Don't. You. Even. I was listening when Roger told you he'd kill your mother if he had to and you went along with it. You didn't back out when he stabbed Mitch with my knife. Don't you *dare* try to tell me you were doing it for Evelyn."

Kevin put his head down on the bar and sobbed.

"I know. I was greedy. And then ... and then I got scared. I thought he would kill me, too, if I didn't go along. And now he's going to anyway."

"He won't, but I might. He's locked up and will be for a long time while I'm here listening to guests complain that you're stealing from them. What did you take from room 113?"

Kevin raised his head and looked at Sheila with wide, red eyes. "He knows? Did you tell Mom?"

"As soon as I do she'll have you sent back to prison where you belong. I'm going to knock on his door before 10:00 PM and if he says it hasn't been returned then I'll tell Evelyn. And the police, just in case one of them doesn't. I won't allow you to do this to her."

This made me very nervous. Kevin was a desperate man and Sheila had backed him into a corner. There was no telling what he might do.

Sheila picked up her rag again and rubbed angrily on the bar top. By now it was clean enough to eat off of but that was no longer why she was rubbing it. She stopped suddenly.

"Why did you say Roger was still going to kill you? He's in prison."

"He can sneak out."

"That's impossible. He's not that clever."

"I got a video on Snapchat. It showed him standing outside the prison and he said he was going to kill me if I didn't change my testimony. He said he'd kill everybody that was testifying."

Sheila lowered her eyes at Kevin. "I don't believe you."

Kevin's left hand dropped from the bar and I saw him reaching for his pocket. Fearing that it might be a gun he was after, I hopped from bar stool to bar stool. I pounced, knocking against Kevin's right arm and spilling his whiskey on his shirt as he pulled out his phone.

"Whiskers! Down!"

Embarrassed, I jumped to the floor. Kevin took off his shirt with the Parrot Eyes Inn logo, revealing a white, sleeveless undershirt.

Just then the door creaked open again.

"Five minutes!" Sheila yelled. She sighed and glared at Kevin. "Show me later. I'll take a break at 9:00. Meet me by the pool."

Kevin nodded and walked out, closing the door behind him.

Kevin's words rang in my head. "He said he'd kill everybody that was testifying." That meant Sheila. And Julia, Becky, and Tarrie Ann. Probably more people in town. I wasn't sure I believed the video was real but I was anxious to see the screenshot. Had Roger found a way to get outside of the prison? If so, no one in Paradise Cove was safe.

FOUR

"It's the smallest details that make the biggest difference. I once uncovered a case where the burglar had made himself a peanut butter and jelly sandwich — I don't know why you Americans love them so much — before leaving with a pillowcase full of jewelry. Even the suspect's wife believed he was guilty so the police were lazy and did a sloppy job. The wife was testifying against her husband, saying that he was out of the house that night, that he had missed his supper, and that he loved a good *PB&J* — not that I concede there is such a thing."

A roar of laughter rose from the large group of star-struck writers surrounding Victor Bloodworth at the bar. I have to admit there was also one star-struck cat. The man could tell a story.

"Anyway, if the prosecutor had stopped there he would have gotten a conviction. Instead, he introduced as state's evidence the peanut butter jar from the crime scene, and the wife, still on the witness stand, says 'Oh, no ... my Jeffrey would never eat *that*. It's crunchy. He only eats *creamy* peanut butter!' His attorney found a dozen witnesses to say the defendant refused to go near crunchy peanut butter and the man was acquitted. Police got back to work and identified some fingermarks as matching another suspect who had been arrested in a separate burglary two weeks later. This suspect had a jar of crunchy peanut butter in his pantry. Crunchy or creamy. It was the difference between freedom and prison."

Victor's audience hung on every word. His stories of police investigations were so vivid, so detailed. The techniques used to catch killers and other criminals were different from anything Fred had taught me. Knowing that Victor made his living, a very good one, by telling stories, I wasn't sure if I could believe him. I also wasn't sure that I cared. Maybe his accent had something to do with it.

Why are stories so much more interesting when told by an Englishman?

"Good evening, all. It's been a pleasure. Don't stay up too late — my presentation on Police Procedures, U.K. vs. U.S. begins in ... twelve hours and three minutes."

Victor shook hands with several admirers on his way out.

I had been so engrossed that I'd forgotten about Sheila's plan to meet Kevin. One of the men who crowded in with us rested his arm on the bar right in front of my face. His watch said two minutes until 9:00. Time for Sheila to take her break. I hopped from my barstool and darted across the floor. Victor said something funny as he stepped out the door causing a man near me to stomp his foot as he laughed. Spray from his wet shoe splashed my fur. I'd heard thunder outside so it was no surprise. But I hate getting my fur wet. If I hadn't been so concerned about Sheila's safety I would have stayed in.

"I've got it. Thanks, Sheila."

Evelyn had arrived and Sheila stepped out from behind the bar. Out in the hallway she leaned against the wall to catch her breath.

"If I still smoked, Whiskers, I'd be pulling out a cigarette right now."

This was a revelation to me. Sheila had never smoked since I'd known her. But then I hadn't known about her bartending days, either, before this summer. I had learned a lot about her since Fred passed. I think she had learned a lot about herself, as well.

"Let's get this over with."

Sheila pushed herself away from the wall and we walked together to the exit by the pool. The wind had blown water under the door and soaked the carpet but when we walked out the rain had stopped. I looked for Kevin. Even with my superior cat vision, I didn't see anyone. I was on high alert, still concerned that he might attack Sheila to keep her from telling Evelyn and the police about what he had done. Umbrellas at the tables flapped in the wind. As we walked further out I noticed there was a stray umbrella on the concrete beside the pool.

A rustling noise behind us got my attention. I turned just as a lone figure rushed past us.

Whoever it was ran to the gate, placed their hands on the top of the fence, and hurdled over. They disappeared into the dark.

With the low light, the surprise, and the speed at which the figure moved I couldn't make out a face or even a hair color for certain. Just that it was a darker color. Yet somehow the figure seemed familiar.

Sheila seemed disoriented by the sudden appearance and disappearance. She stumbled to a table and sat down on a wet chair, rising briefly when she noticed her bottom was soaked then sighing and sitting back down. I walked over and rubbed against her leg. It sometimes soothes her when she is upset.

"What an unusual thing, Whiskers. Where do you suppose they were going in such a hurry?"

"Away from us," I meowed. "Whoever that was, they didn't want to be seen out here. The question is why?"

"Of course, I'll give you a belly rub."

Sheila, misunderstanding me as always, reached down and placed me in her lap. Her fingers tickled my belly, making my whole body tingle and destroying my concentration. I heard Karen Carpenter singing "Close to You" and my eyes closed. Not a good time to be distracted as we were expecting Kevin at any moment but I was powerless.

Then Sheila stopped.

Her hand lay motionless on my belly and her whole body seemed to tense.

"Whiskers. Is that ... ?"

I opened my eyes and reoriented myself. Hopping onto the wet table, I rushed to find a dry spot then followed Sheila's gaze to the pool where a man lay face down, motionless, in the water. He wore black pants and a white sleeveless undershirt. Kevin.

"You haven't touched anything, have you?"

Chief Anderson looked at Sheila with his eyebrows lowered.

"No."

"You didn't call your murder club friends over to snoop around first?"

"Of course not, Chief. Everything here is exactly like I found it. Except his body has floated. It was closer to the ... "

The police chief waved Sheila off and turned back to his crime scene. It was illuminated now with all of the lights on. Kevin's body floated on the far side. I could see red and white stripes across the umbrella on the concrete now. Most of the windows facing the pool were open with one or more curious guests looking down. Evelyn had been taken back inside after collapsing at the sight of her dead son. Officer Reid was following my friend Kojak, the K-9 officer, around the perimeter of the pool area.

Chief Anderson returned his attention to Sheila.

"Tell me again why you were out here."

"I was supposed to meet Kevin. He had something he wanted to show me."

"Something?" Chief Anderson turned back to face Sheila. "That's a pretty vague statement. Care to elaborate?"

Sheila took a deep breath and slowly released it. "A picture. Or video. A screenshot from a video." She paused. "Of Roger."

"Roger that tried to frame you for murder? Roger that Kevin was supposed to testify against? *That* Roger?"

"Yes. That Roger."

Sheila sat quietly. Chief Anderson harrumphed and waited expectantly.

"Oh, come on. This is like pulling teeth. *Why* was Kevin going to show you a picture of Roger?"

"Because he said Roger was threatening him. Kevin told me that Roger sent him a video on SnapTalk that ... "

"Snap CHAT?"

"Yes, that sounds right. Roger sent a video saying he was going to kill Kevin. And everybody else that was supposed to testify against him."

The chief rolled his eyes. "Unlikely. The prison would never let him have a phone to send messages from."

"That's the thing."

"What's the thing?"

"Roger wasn't in prison. According to Kevin, the video showed Roger standing *outside* the prison."

"That's ridiculous."

"That's what I said. And now here we are."

Sheila looked at Kevin's body which Officer Reid was finally pulling from the water with a long-handled net. Several clicks could be heard from the surrounding windows as guests used their phones to snap pictures.

Chief Anderson glared upward and a few windows slammed shut.

"This person that you saw fleeing the scene. Describe them for me."

"I didn't get a look at his face — I'm pretty sure it was a man, they were wearing men's clothing. A golf shirt and pants with a pair of gloves sticking out of the back pocket. Just like ... "

"Just like what?"

"Just like Roger always dressed."

Chief Anderson closed his eyes and his jaw clenched.

Officer Reid had retrieved Kevin's body which now sat on the concrete next to the steps at the end. "You want me to empty his pockets?"

Chief Anderson spun on his heels and walked over, seemingly glad to get away from Sheila for a moment. I followed and quietly made my way to where Kojak was sitting.

"Not now, Whiskers," Kojak growled.

"Just point to anything you found," I quietly meowed.

Kojak pointed his nose toward the door we had entered the pool area from. The mystery figure must have been hiding in the dark corner there. On the edge of a planter was a coffee cup. I stepped to the nearest wall and crawled along the edge to investigate.

A Sea Brews logo was on the coffee cup. Thanks to more than one frustrated outburst from Sheila, I was well aware that Sea Brews closed early in the afternoon so the coffee couldn't have been fresh at the time of the murder. It probably had been sitting there most of the day, waiting to be cleaned up.

Except ... One thing bothered me. The cup was dry. Not the inside — I couldn't see that because of the plastic lid. There was no rain on the cup other than at the bottom where it touched the planter.

Everything around the cup was wet but the paper cup itself wasn't. Which told me that it had been placed there after the rain stopped, just shortly before we came outside and discovered Kevin's body. Kojak had done well to notice it. Why did someone bring a cold or empty cup of coffee out here?

The killer, if that's who it was that ran off, had probably been standing in this very spot, waiting for something or someone. I closed my eyes and tried to remember the details. Something about the incident was bothering me but I couldn't quite put my paw on it. I thought back to the first indication of trouble. A rustling noise behind us. Then it all went so quickly. The person ran past us, crossed the pool area to the gate, placed their hands on the fence, and ... wait. That was it. Their hands were dark. This person was wearing gloves. That was weird because Sheila had noticed gloves hanging out of their back pocket. Why would they have two sets of gloves?

I would have to figure that out later. Kevin's pockets had been emptied and I wanted to get a look before the contents disappeared into evidence bags. I retraced my steps along the wall's edge then hopped up on another wet table to get a better view. Too bad the umbrellas had been put down before the rain.

Chief Anderson was looking through a wallet but not finding anything interesting. Next to Kevin's body, I saw a set of keys, a USB drive, and the phone he had pulled out in the bar. Everything was soaked so I wondered if the USB drive and phone would be ruined. They would at least need to dry out before being plugged in.

What about Victor's stolen property? Had Kevin returned it or did he still have it? If it was on his person then the most likely item was the USB drive. I recognized the phone as Kevin's, the keys looked like hotel keys, and if the wallet had belonged to anyone other than Kevin the chief would have said something when he looked inside. There could be something in there that had been stolen but my best bet was the USB drive. Which begged the question, what was on it?

I could also see now that Kevin had a gash on the side of his head. Not much blood but he'd been hit pretty hard by something.

"Whaddya think, chief?"

Chief Anderson rubbed his chin and considered Officer Reid's question.

"Accident."

"Ya think?"

"I do. See the umbrella over there? The wind picked it up and blew it to the edge of the pool where the victim was standing. It knocked him in the head, he fell in and drowned. Case closed."

Sheila rushed over to confront the chief. "Case Closed? Surely you can't be serious?"

"I am serious ... and don't call me Shirley." Chief Anderson chuckled to himself.

Sheila was not amused.

"Don't worry. We'll bag up all the evidence and take a look. Reid, make sure ya get everything. Even that coffee cup yer dog was sniffin' at. Just to be safe."

Chief Anderson's theory had some merit. It had been windy, especially earlier when the storm came through. But the umbrellas had been pulled down and tied off so the wind wouldn't have been able to pick them up. The one on the concrete was partially open but probably just because the strap had come undone when the killer swung it at Kevin. I looked around to see which table it had come from. There were red and white striped umbrellas in the middle of every table. None were missing. So where had it come from?

Chief Anderson was wrong but how could I show him? I screeched, making the noise that always gets humans' attention. They hate it.

"What?" Kojak barked at me.

"The tables. They all have umbrellas." I ran from one table to the next, jumping up and rubbing against the umbrella at the center of each one. Guests laughed from their windows.

"Your cat's gone mad, Sheila."

"No crazier than you, Chief, if you believe this was an accident. How do you explain the person who ran away and jumped over the fence?"

"All I know," the chief growled, "is that it wasn't Roger."

FIVE

"It's so good of you to help. Evelyn needs it."

Sheila waited for Jimmy to place the last of his tools on the back of her golf cart. He had so many there was no place for me in my normal spot. I liked to ride in the back where golf clubs were supposed to go. Sheila didn't play golf so my spot was normally secure. On this trip, I would be riding on her lap. Jimmy, dressed in blue jeans and a denim shirt instead of his normal fishing clothes, sat in the passenger seat.

"Sorry I'm bringing so much. I just don't know what I'll need."

"Everything," I meowed.

Sheila reached down with one hand to scratch my chin while she drove with the other hand. "Of course, Whiskers. As you wish, Whiskers."

"You spoil that cat," Jimmy said, laughing.

He reached over to pet me but I hissed at him. "Mind your own business, pal!"

Sheila slowed as she turned a corner. Jimmy reached back and put a hand on his pile of tools to keep it steady.

"You should probably start with the elevator. It's nothing mechanical. I think it's just the button that calls it down to the lobby. Several wood trim pieces need to be reattached in the hallways. Some tiles need replacing. Paint, carpet, light fixtures ... "

"I get the picture! I'm worn out already and we're not even there yet. But I'm glad to fix whatever I can. I don't know what this town would be like without the Parrot Eyes Inn."

"Unfortunately, we might soon find out. Evelyn was struggling already. I'm not sure she can recover, no matter how much we get fixed. But if we can at least get her through this conference then she can focus on burying her son."

We all sat silently for the rest of the ride.

Sheila pulled into a parking space by the back door of the Inn and got out.

"Can I help with the tools?"

"No, thanks. I'll leave them here for now, if that's okay, and take a look first. See where I need to start."

The exit door opened. Julia was stepping out backward, pushing the door with her backside and carrying a trash bag in each hand. Her neon-colored outfit looked like it came straight out of a Richard Simmons workout video from the 1980s.

Sheila snorted.

"I heard that," Julia said without looking in our direction. The snort was all she needed to identify Sheila. She walked toward the dumpster. "Tarrie Ann is looking for you. She needs the key to the bar."

Jimmy caught the door before it closed and held it open for Sheila.

"The bar doesn't open for hours. Why does she need … ?"

Now Julia stopped and looked at Sheila. "Seriously?"

"Oh. Yeah. Pretend I didn't ask that."

Julia tossed the bags into the dumpster and walked back inside with Sheila. I hurried forward expecting to have to rush in as the door closed but Jimmy waited for me.

"Take your time, Whiskers."

"Very kind of you," I meowed. I was starting to understand why Zappa and Blue liked Jimmy so much. It wasn't just the fish he shared with them. He noticed animals in a way that most humans never did. Even Buster, that drooling ball of fur and energy. Jimmy had adopted him after his human died.

Becky, looking as sharp as ever in a black pantsuit, waved at us from behind the reception desk as we walked into the lobby. Or rather, she waved at Julia with a sense of urgency. A thin woman in a white skirt and blouse was standing in front of the desk with her hands on her hips.

"It's a good thing for you that this hotel doesn't have a website," the woman was saying. "If I had been able to see it, I never would have come!"

I finally recognized her as Buffy, the woman who had made Isabella cry the previous day. I still didn't know what Isabella had been accused of.

Becky held a fake smile. "Julia will be right up with a fresh set of sheets, won't you Julia?"

Buffy turned and looked at Julia. Her eyes moved slowly down, taking in Julia's entire outfit and grimacing. "If you don't have silk then 100% cotton will do, I suppose. As long as it's a decent thread count."

The office door opened and Isabella walked out. Chief Anderson's voice followed her.

"We'll let you know if we have any other questions."

Buffy leaned in toward Becky conspiratorially and said "I hope they asked her why the victim was in her room yesterday." She spoke just loud enough to be overheard.

Isabella spun around and faced Buffy. "If you think you know something just go ahead and say it!"

The two women stared daggers at each other for an uncomfortably long time.

"I didn't think so," Isabella said then spun again and strutted out of the lobby into the hallway.

"She's had one successful book," Buffy said once it was safe, "and everyone says she stole that one. That's why the man was in her room, she was paying him to steal a manuscript from one of us. I'd bet my father's yacht on it."

Chief Anderson stuck his head out of the office door.

"I don't believe we've gotten a statement from you, ma'am. Care to join me?"

"Not a good time, officer. I'm late for Victor's session." Buffy walked away in a hurry.

"*Chief*," Chief Anderson grumbled. He addressed Sheila. "See? I'm investigating, just like I said I would. You haven't seen Roger around, have you?" he added sarcastically. He started to close the office door before noticing Officer Reid at the hotel entrance, struggling with an office chair. After a couple of failed attempts, the large leather chair made it through.

"In here," Chief Anderson directed. "About time. This cheap old chair is about to ruin my back."

Officer Reid rolled the chair past the front desk and into the office, again struggling to make it fit through the doorway.

Jimmy frowned. "Why did he ask you about Roger?"

Sheila stood quietly for a moment. "Because I told him the killer looked like Roger."

Jimmy squinted his eyes and cocked his head. "But it couldn't be him. He's in prison."

"Supposed to be." Sheila filled him in on the events of the previous night, which she'd already told Julia, Becky, and Tarrie Ann.

Jimmy listened carefully but didn't look convinced. "I can't explain what you saw but it sounds to me like this Isabella is a more likely suspect. Why would Kevin have gone to her room?"

I had a theory on that. We already knew that Kevin had stolen something from Victor. And we knew that a USB drive was found in Kevin's pocket. The USB drive could have contained Victor's new manuscript and Isabella was suspected of stealing and publishing someone else's story before. Buffy was convinced that was

Isabella's reason for being at the conference. To steal a story. But if she paid Kevin to steal Victor's story then why would she kill him before she got it? Or was it Victor who killed him, trying to keep Isabella from getting the story even though he told Sheila he would wait?

Becky pulled a room key out from under the desk and held it out to Jimmy.

"If you think Isabella did it, then take a look around while you're in her room, Mr. Handy Man. She says her air conditioner isn't working."

SIX

"Maintenance. Is anyone in the room?"

Jimmy knocked again and waited a few seconds before using the key card Becky had given him to access Isabella's room. The light turned green and he turned the knob.

As Jimmy opened the door, I saw another door down the hall open and Max stepped out into the hall.

"Wow. Another one? That room has more guys going in it than the men's bathroom downstairs."

Jimmy stopped and looked toward the voice. "Excuse me?"

Max just laughed as he stepped into the elevator and disappeared.

Jimmy reached down and picked up his toolbox then held the door open for me. "After you, detective." The air inside was noticeably warmer than in the hall. The room was tidy, at least as far as I could tell from my vantage point on the floor. A pair of slippers sat side by side near the foot of the queen-sized bed. The curtains were open and, after hopping up on the window sill, I looked down at the pool where we had discovered Kevin's body.

Jimmy walked to the unit underneath the window. It was silent. He set his toolbox on the floor. After taking a couple of minutes examining all the visible parts he stepped back around the bed to the opposite wall and inspected the thermostat.

"There's no way it's 72 degrees in here," he stated. Jimmy pulled the cover off of the thermostat and set it down on the bed. "What's this?"

I hopped up on the bed to see what had caught his attention. Someone had printed out a website article claiming that Isabella had stolen the story for her bestselling novel from another author.

Written in large red letters across the page were the words "Go home thief!"

Jimmy picked up the paper and began to read the article silently. And slowly. I impatiently waited for my turn which never came.

A sudden voice from the doorway caused Jimmy to drop the paper.

"Buffy did that. I recognize the bright red lipstick she wrote it with."

Isabella had returned to her room and busted us snooping. I jumped off the bed.

"Are you going to fix my air conditioner, too, or just go through my stuff?"

Jimmy's face turned as red as the lipstick on the paper.

"Sorry, I set the thermostat cover beside it, and ... "

Isabella picked up the paper, wadded it into a ball, and dropped it in the trash can.

"Max told me someone was in my room. Actually, he announced to the whole conference that 'yet another man' was in my room. Didn't I see you talking to Buffy in the lobby a few minutes ago?"

"I'm surprised you didn't slap her. Why does she hate you so much?"

"Just jealous. Her daddy's rich and he bought a publishing company to get her a book deal but even with all of his help nobody bought her books. I was already signed with that company and when my book took off they moved all of their publicity efforts to me."

"I can see where that would make somebody jealous."

"Yeah, but she needs to get over it. The anonymous source in that article claiming I stole my story? It was her. That made Daddy mad so he sent me on the book-signing tour he had set up for her. Fancy restaurants and five-star hotels you wouldn't believe. They even have working air conditioning." Isabella gave Jimmy a playful smirk.

"I'll have that fixed in a minute. The thermostat just needs to be calibrated." Jimmy walked over to his toolbox by the window.

"Thanks. That other guy said he'd be back to do it but obviously that's not gonna happen. Do they know who killed him yet?"

Jimmy shook his head. "Not yet." He grabbed a screwdriver and started fiddling with the thermostat.

"Well, they need to figure it out soon before the stories get out of control. You realize who we all are, right? A dead body in the middle of a murder mystery writer conference is just too tempting to resist."

"Who do the other writers think did it?"

Isabella looked Jimmy straight in the eyes. "Me."

Well, that was quite the confession. She hadn't admitted to the crime but confessing that her fellow writers suspected her was a bold move.

Jimmy didn't seem to know how to respond.

"What about your lady friends in the Paradise Cove Murder Society? Do they think I did it, too? Is that why you're here? "

Now I was as stunned as Jimmy who still was speechless. How did she know about the ladies and their investigations?

"Oh, yes. You know we're not going to miss something like that. Especially when it's someone in the society who finds the body. I'm thinking about putting them in my next book."

The air conditioner kicked on and cool air started pouring into the room.

"That should do it," Jimmy said, picking up the thermostat cover and setting it back in place. He put his screwdriver back in his toolbox, shut the lid, and started toward the door, anxious to get out of the conversation. I stood up on the carpet and walked behind him.

"Is that a police badge on your cat's collar? Are you helping the ladies in the club or are you working for the police?" Isabella was enjoying teasing Jimmy.

Jimmy stopped and turned around to face her. "You told me the others think you killed Kevin. Did you?"

"I thought you'd never ask. No. I haven't killed anyone except in my books."

"See anything from your window? You've got a great view of the crime scene."

Isabella laughed. "I wasn't in my room. Buffy's theatrics got under my skin so I took a quiet walk on the beach. By myself. And, no, I don't have any witnesses to corroborate that so you can tell the ladies to keep me on their list of possible suspects."

"I'll do that. Who do you think did it? Buffy?"

Isabella laughed out loud. "She'll stab you in the back figuratively, but actual murder? No, it's not her style. If I were going to investigate somebody it would be Max. He's been obsessed with me since I rejected him in the lobby. He was stalking me when Kevin came to fix my AC and maybe he got the wrong idea. He could have killed him in a jealous rage. He saw you coming in, too, so ... you might want to be careful."

"I'll keep that in mind."

Something about the way she said that sounded less like a sincere warning and more like a threat. But that could have been my imagination. We cats are a suspicious bunch.

Jimmy walked out and I followed, holding my head up to make sure my badge was clearly visible on my chest.

SEVEN

"She told you to watch your back?"

Jimmy and I had returned to the lobby where Tarrie Ann had replaced Becky at the front desk. Sheila was sorting through paperwork next to her. The rest of the lobby was empty for the moment. I had found a comfy chair next to the plastic palm tree.

"Not in those exact words, but she told me to be careful. She made it sound like Max might come after me. She thinks he's so obsessed with her that he might be taking out the competition."

Tarrie Ann snickered. "Are you competition for Isabella's affections?"

Sheila stopped flipping through papers and looked at Jimmy.

Jimmy's face turned red again. "I am NOT!" He carried his toolbox to the elevator to examine the faulty call button - and to get away from the teasing ladies.

The doors to the conference room opened down the hall and several attendees walked out. Max emerged from the crowd and approached the desk. He was waving something in his right hand as he walked."

"Batteries? This remote control for the projector is dying and my talk on creating a new identity starts in 15 minutes."

Sheila held out her hand and accepted the remote from him. She rummaged through a drawer behind the desk, found a battery, swapped it out for the old one, and gave the remote back to Max who strutted away without saying anything more.

"You're welcome," Tarrie Ann mumbled under her breath.

Sheila snorted then turned away, hiding her face, when Jimmy glanced back in their direction.

I was watching Max head down the hall. He was about the same size and shape as whoever had run past us the previous night at the pool. Tarrie Ann was apparently thinking the same thing.

"What do you think, Sheila?"

"About what?"

"Could Max have been the person you saw right before you found Kevin's body?"

Sheila turned back around and looked down the hall just in time to see Max walk through a group of conference attendees and into the conference room.

"Maybe. He and Roger are a similar build."

"You don't believe Roger did it, do you?"

"I don't know what to think. But Kevin said Roger was going to kill him. Then he died and someone who looked like Roger ran away from the scene. What would you think?" Sheila's voice cracked as she asked the question. The stress was getting to her.

Tarrie Ann put her hand on Sheila's shoulder. "I think we need to keep an open mind. Whoever it was, we'll catch him. We're the Paradise Cove Murder Society and we haven't missed one yet!"

Chief Anderson stepped out of Evelyn's office. "*I think you need to let the professionals handle this. I'm interviewing everyone and *if this was a murder*, I'll catch the killer. You ladies have enough on your hands trying to run a hotel."

The chief ignored the nasty looks from Sheila, Tarrie Ann, and me. He walked to the front door. "I've got a lunch meeting I need to prepare for and then Max is next on my list," he said as he left the building.

I quietly hopped down from my seat by the palm tree and padded into Evelyn's office. Chief Anderson's leather chair was situated behind the desk. I could see why he had Officer Reid bring it down. It looked very expensive and when I jumped up on it, it felt comfortable. I squatted, peed on the seat, and left the office without being noticed.

The writers in the hallway had started making their way back into the conference room. Tarrie Ann decided she would join them.

"Can you watch the desk, Sheila? There shouldn't be much happening since they're all in the session and all the rooms are booked. I want to watch this Max guy and see what he's about."

"Sure. Have at it."

Max had said his session was about creating a new identity. That was too good to miss. A chance to investigate a suspect and learn about how criminals worked at the same time? Count me in! I walked with Tarrie Ann down the hall and we snuck in with the last of the attendees.

The conference room was set up with several round tables and eight chairs at each table. A long table was at the front of the room with Max sitting at one end and a projector in the middle. The screen hanging from the ceiling displayed a PowerPoint slide with the title "Creating a New Identity For Your Characters: How to Get a Fake Social Security Card, Driver's License, and Passport. Presenter: Maximus Sharp."

Tarrie Ann looked around for an empty seat near the back but they were all full. Victor Bloodworth noticed and stood up, motioning for her to take his seat next to Isabella. I thought he'd move to one of the open seats at the front but instead, he quietly walked out and closed the conference room door behind him. That seemed odd, but maybe he already knew how to get fake IDs. He'd written enough books so it had probably come up in his research before.

Max stood up and cleared his throat. The room got quiet.

"Who here has ever had a character in their book who needed to disappear?"

Almost everybody raised a hand.

"The lazy way to write this is to just have another character say 'I know a guy' and then set up a transaction. But that leaves witnesses and it doesn't give your readers any insight into how these fake documents get created. Today I'm going to show you the process that real criminals use to create a new identity for themselves."

And that's when it all went to ... well — you know.

Max pushed a button on the remote control and a new slide showed up on the screen displaying the website for the Social Security Administration. Then he set the remote down, picked up a laser pointer, and directed it to the point on the screen that said "card and record."

As you may recall, I am a cat. And you know, or should know, that laser pointers hold a magic power over cats. That red dot is just irresistible. We *have* to catch it. So, while Max was showing his audience where to go on the website, I ran between several tables, leaped onto the front table, and launched myself at the screen like a lion attacking a gazelle on the African savannah.

Max, shocked by my sudden appearance, dropped his arm which sent the red dot flying to the floor near his feet. I followed it, clawing at the carpet as he backed up, jerking the laser pointer in every direction. The dot moved into the crowd and, completely helpless to control myself, I jumped onto one of the tables, knocking over at least two glasses of water and causing Buffy, who had been seated at the table, to scream. Her scream got Max's attention and as he looked at her the red dot appeared again on the front of her dress. I heard Isabella laughing from the back table. My legs were primed and ready to send me straight at Buffy when one of the men at the table pulled the laser pointer out of Max's hand and the dot disappeared.

I was frozen. Humiliated. Tarrie Ann reached out to grab me and I managed to move again. I darted toward the conference room door which Sheila opened, coming in to check on the noise. Running past her, I entered the hallway and kept running. Fortunately, Jimmy had gone out to get some more tools and I was able to make it out the back door. I didn't stop running until I was home. Bursting through the cat flap I went immediately to my special cushion on the shelf — the one made from Fred's old uniform.

As I sat down, air was pushed out from inside the cushion and I caught a faint whiff of Fred's scent. I couldn't stand it. The man I had looked up to, who taught me everything I knew about detective work. I had just completely disgraced myself and the reminder of his patience and professionalism was just too much. I hopped back down, went through the pet door again, and slunk away into the dunes.

EIGHT

"Give yourself a break, man. No cat can resist the red dot, man."

You find out who your friends are when you're down and Zappa was proving himself to be a good friend. I hadn't brought him any catnip on this visit but he was still giving me a pep talk. We were both stretched out on our backs in the sand, soaking in the sunshine.

"How many killers you caught? At least three that I know of. Man, that's a big deal. And you saved that one lady who was about to drink that poison drink. You're the best cop I know."

"How many cops do you know, Zappa?"

"Besides you? Uh, none. But that's what makes you so great. Most cops wouldn't give a cat like me the time of day. Here you are, layin' out with me in the sand, shootin' the breeze. You're one cool cat, Detective Whiskers."

"Thanks."

"No prob, man. Hey — you seen Jimmy? Normally he'd be out here fishin' by now."

"Yeah, I don't think he's gonna make it today. They've got him busy fixing things at the Inn. It would take him the rest of the year to fix every-thing that needs fixing there."

Zappa turned onto his side and looked at me. "The rest of the year?"

I laughed. "Don't worry. He's just trying to get them through this conference, then I'm sure he'll be back out here catching plenty of fish for you and Blue. You think you can make it a couple of days?"

Zappa rolled back over and stared up into the sky again without answering.

"Speaking of Blue," I added, "you talk to her lately?"

"Nah, man. She's been keepin' to herself. Like she usually does."

Blue wasn't the most social of creatures. I never saw her much with other birds, even, let alone cats and people. The more I saw how much she kept to herself, the more I realized how lucky I was that she tolerated me. She was probably wondering about Jimmy, too.

"Maybe I better go check on her. Let her know she's gonna have to catch her own dinner."

"Good talkin' to ya, man. Don't get distracted by any red dots on the way."

Zappa laughed, but it was a friendly laugh. It was good to be reminded that it's okay for me to be a cat. I mean, that's who I've always been and I couldn't change that if I wanted to. It doesn't mean I can't be a great detective. I've just got my little quirks like anybody else. Adrian Monk. Now there's a detective with some weird behaviors but he always caught the bad guy. Sheila and I loved watching Monk on TV. I was always rooting for him to get his badge back.

I stepped out of the dunes and saw Blue standing at the edge of the water near the pier. As I walked toward her I made sure to make myself known. She doesn't like anyone sneaking up on her.

"Hey, Blue," I said from a good distance away. She turned to face me and didn't move so I kept walking toward her. "Just thought I'd let you know Jimmy's not gonna be fishing today."

Blue turned back to face the water. I stepped up beside her but not too close.

"He's helping fix some things at the Parrot Eyes Inn. He might be there a couple of days so you and Zappa will have to fend for yourselves."

"Thanks for letting me know."

She lowered her gaze and started scanning the water for any fish nearby.

"At least that means Buster's not around, making all that noise and chasing things. I know he gets under your skin. Or feathers."

Blue didn't react at first, just kept scanning the water until she suddenly drove her pointy beak down. She came back up with a small fish which she ate.

"Looks like you'll be fine. Anyway, just wanted to let you know. I hope you're doing okay."

Blue nodded slightly. I turned to go back to the house.

"How about Zappa?" Blue asked.

I stopped and looked back. "He doesn't seem too worried, as long as Jimmy's not gone more than a couple of days. If he is, we'll figure something out."

I continued walking back home. As I reached the boardwalk I noticed a shadow in the sand and looked up to see Blue flying away. She had another small fish in her beak and as she flew over the dunes she dropped it into the sand near where I'd left Zappa.

My walk on the beach had done the trick. My little embarrassment at the convention wasn't nearly as bad as I had made it out to be. When you've got good friends, like I do, you can get over things like that. Time for me to get back to work.

I poked my head through the pet door and heard a scratching noise. A gray blur streaked across the floor from the kitchen toward a tiny crack on the side wall of the living room.

"It's just me, Roddy. Nothing to worry about." I made my way inside.

The blur stopped right before reaching the wall. Roddy was a mouse that lived with us, although Sheila didn't know about it. As long as she didn't know, everything was fine. Roddy and I had a deal. He only ate scraps off the floor and kept things clean. I left him alone. Some would say I was derelict in my duties as a cat, but the way I saw it, Roddy had been living here in Sunset Cottage since before Sheila and I arrived. As long as we were able to peacefully coexist, I didn't see any harm.

"You scared me. I thought you left with Sheila."

"I did. I came back without her because ... well, it doesn't matter. You're looking good."

"I am?" Roddy looked at his body.

"You've lost weight."

"Oh." Roddy sounded disappointed. "Yeah, we mice don't really look at that the same way as people do. A skinny mouse is just one that can't find enough food. Your human hasn't been leaving me many crumbs lately. Ever since her grandson left it's been slim pickings."

"I smelled something by the house next door. Careful, though, if you go looking for food outside.

Jimmy's not fishing for a couple of days so Zappa might be hungry."

Roddy's face dropped. "Thanks for the warning!" He slipped back inside the wall.

I drank some water from my bowl and then started walking back to the Inn. This murder wasn't gonna solve itself. And I wanted to be there when Chief Anderson sat down in his chair.

NINE

Max had just wrapped up his session when I returned. I snuck under a table, doing my best to not be noticed. The attendees were heading out in a hurry to get lunch. Tarrie Ann made her way to the front and was greeted by Max who, thankfully, was not holding the laser pointer. She spoke with a sugary sweet voice.

"I was hoping you'd have some books for sale. I wanted to get you to sign one for me."

Max grinned from ear to ear and stole a quick look at Tarrie Ann's curvy body. She looked much younger than she was and never failed to catch the attention of the men around her, even the ones too young to recognize her as a former television star.

"It's not really that kind of conference, but I do happen to have a copy of my first book in my room. I'd be happy to give it to you. What room are you staying in?"

Smooth. He'd already asked for her room number less than 10 seconds after meeting her.

"Oh, I'm not a guest here. I'm helping my friend who owns the Inn since she just lost her son. Could you leave it at the front desk?"

Max's grin faded. "You're part of that group, aren't you? The ladies who decided to become detectives?"

"The Paradise Cove Murder Society. We've solved three murders already and we'll find out who killed Evelyn's son, too." Tarrie Ann's voice had a little edge to it. She clearly didn't care for the way Max dismissed their group but she kept her smile. "Some people seem to think you did it, but you don't look like a killer to me."

"By *some people* I imagine you mean Isabella? That crazy woman thinks I'm obsessed with her just because I complimented her body when we met. Did you ask her why the victim came to her room shortly before he died? She was expecting him, too. When she opened the door she said 'Thank God. I am so hot,' and practically dragged him inside." Max rolled his eyes. "He wasn't in there long. Must have been disappointing."

"He was there to fix the air conditioner."

"Oh." Max nodded. "That makes sense, I guess."

"And you just happened to be in the hallway when he arrived?"

Max turned defensive. "Come on now! Did she say I was stalking her? My room is just a couple of doors down. I was having a hard time getting my key card to work. That's why I was in the hall."

"And you were still trying to unlock your door when he left?"

"Um. No. I, uh ... I went back out to get some ice."

"So just good timing, then?"

"I guess so."

Tarrie Ann pulled out her phone and dictated a note in a sarcastic voice. "Suspect Max says he just happened to be in the hall when victim entered and left Isabella's room. Not stalking her at all." She stopped the dictation and started to put her phone away then brought it back up near her face. "Or does Isabella have it all wrong and you were *actually* stalking the *victim*?" She pointed the phone toward Max.

Max's eyes got wide. "Where do you get off calling me a suspect? How about your friend who conveniently found the body and saw some ghost running from the scene that nobody else saw? Didn't she have a history with the victim? I heard he tried to frame her for murder. I bet she wasn't happy to see him walking around again. Shouldn't she be the number one suspect? I'm being interviewed by the real police in a few minutes. I think I'll mention that to the chief."

It did seem strange that Chief Anderson hadn't already pointed a finger a Sheila. Maybe he was afraid to after already being proved wrong about both her and her grandson on previous cases. But that might change if Max pushed the issue. Perhaps Tarrie Ann needed to back off but she didn't look like she was about to so I intervened. I walked out from under the table and meowed hello.

"What is that cat doing in here again?"

I walked up to Tarrie Ann and rubbed against her leg. She picked me up. "There you are, Whiskers. I'd better get you back to Sheila. She's worried sick about you."

Max picked up his laser pointer and put it in his leather messenger bag along with several other items that had been scattered on the table. "Thanks for coming to my session. I hope you learned something," he said sarcastically.

"I did. But I'd still like that book if you don't mind."

Tarrie Ann walked out, carrying me in her arms. As we approached the front desk in the lobby, Sheila looked up from some papers. Her eyes, when she saw Tarrie Ann carrying me, lit up in relief and happiness which were soon replaced by anger and frustration.

"Whiskers! Where have you been and what got into you?"

I pleaded my case, knowing how little good it would do. "It was the red dot, Sheila. No cat can resist it."

"No, you will *not* get a treat!"

She couldn't stay mad at me, though, and reached out to take me from Tarrie Ann. Within seconds her fingers were rubbing my belly. The other thing I am helpless against. I didn't even try to fight it. I just relaxed and let her work her magic.

I was so enraptured by Sheila's belly rub that I didn't even notice Chief Anderson returning from lunch.

"Have y'all seen that Sharp fella?"

Sheila stopped scratching my belly and stared at the chief with a confused look. Officer Reid and Kojak walked in behind him.

I jumped down and found a dark corner underneath the desk.

"Max Sharp," Chief Anderson explained. "He's the next person I'm interviewing."

"On my way," Max answered from the hallway. I could see him through the gap between the desk and the floor. He was walking casually in our direction with his messenger bag hanging from his shoulder.

I couldn't see Chief Anderson but I heard his footsteps as he strode into Evelyn's office. His chair squeaked just a little as he rolled it back and then sat down. It only took a second before he felt and smelled the wet surprise I had left for him.

"What the ... ?" The chief's angry voice echoed out of the office and through the lobby. "Where is that cat!?" he screamed.

I heard footsteps again, heavier this time, rushing out of the office.

"Officer Reid! You and your dog search this hotel until you find that cat. I want him in a cage!"

"You can't ... " Sheila started to object then stopped herself. From under the desk, I could feel the icy glare she was getting.

Max walked past the desk toward the office. "I'll just ... wait in here, shall I?"

Nobody paid him any attention. I could see the chief now, out in the middle of the lobby, pulling the seat of his pants away from his body with one hand and holding his nose with the other. Officer Reid led Kojak over and had him sniff the pants then gave the command to search.

"Let go of his lead!" Chief Anderson barked. "I don't care what he does to that cat!"

Kojak took off, sniffing around the room. He approached the desk and growled in a low voice.

"You've gone too far this time, Whiskers."

I held my tongue as Kojak walked away leading Officer Reid out of the lobby and down the hall.

Chief Anderson trudged back to Evelyn's office. "Mr. Sharp, thank you for meeting with me. This won't take long." He closed the door but I could hear the squeaky wheels of Evelyn's old chair being rolled back behind her desk. Only seconds later the door opened again.

"Somebody's been in my office. Who left these gloves on top of my notebook?"

I wanted to move out from under the front desk and take a look but I couldn't risk it. The chief would kill me if he could, but Kojak would also be in trouble for not finding me when I was so close by.

"You mean Evelyn's office?" Sheila replied.

"Whatever. Did one of you ladies put these on the desk?"

"Not me," said Tarrie Ann. "Maybe it was Whiskers?"

Sheila snorted. She composed herself and asked if she could take a look. Chief Anderson handed them to her.

"They look like the gloves in the back pocket of the man I saw running away from the pool last night."

Chief Anderson groaned. "Well, who put them on the desk? They weren't there when I left for lunch. You've been here this whole time, haven't you? Surely you saw whoever walked into the office?"

"I have been, but I didn't … "

"Actually," Tarrie Ann interjected, "you haven't been here the whole time. You went to the conference room when Whiskers went crazy. Was anybody watching the front desk then?"

Sheila paused. "Nobody. But it was just for a couple of minutes."

Nobody said anything for a moment then Tarrie Ann added, "I know who might have done it."

TEN

Sheila and Chief Anderson stared at Tarrie Ann, waiting for her to reveal who she thought could have snuck into Evelyn's office and left the gloves on the desk. I was interested, too, and crept to the edge of the desk I was hiding under. I could just see everyone but hoped the shadows would keep me hidden.

"I think all of the attendees were in the conference room for Max's session. It was definitely crowded."

Max spoke up from inside the office. "That's right. I counted heads right before I started and everybody was there."

"But did you count me? I was in there and I'm not registered for the conference."

Max walked out of the office. "You're right. I counted the exact number so if you were there that means someone was missing."

"And I know who." Tarrie Ann wore a smug grin. "The older gentleman that everyone seems to gravitate around. He was sitting next to Isabella."

Chief Anderson sighed. "You just said he wasn't there and now you're saying he was. Which is it?"

Tarrie Ann gave him a look. "Both. He was there, but he got up and offered me his seat. I thought he would move to an empty seat up front but instead, he quietly left the room."

Chief Anderson pulled a soggy sheet of paper from his back pocket. He grimaced and carefully unfolded it with the tips of his fingers, trying not to get his hands wet. "Who would that be? What's his name?"

Max answered. "Victor. Victor Bloodworth. Did he really walk out of my presentation?"

Tarrie Ann nodded. "That was Victor? I wish I'd known. He's the writer I wanted to meet!"

Max pouted.

"So he could have snuck into Evelyn's office while I was away," Sheila said. "It must have been him."

"No. It couldn't be." Max seemed certain. "Maybe Victor could have put the gloves on the desk but didn't you say the person you saw at the pool jumped over the gate? There's no way Victor did that. Not at his age. He sometimes looks as if he can barely walk straight."

Sheila started to respond but Max wasn't finished. He turned to face Chief Anderson.

"I don't get why you're focusing your investigation on us writers. Why in the world would we kill a hotel employee? He didn't mean anything to us. Now, your witness here who found the body ... " He pointed at Sheila. "Have you questioned her? She had a motive. The victim, as I understand it, tried to frame her for murder not long ago. She couldn't have been happy to see him back in town. She arranged a secret meeting with him alone at the pool where he died. She was working the front desk by herself when the gloves showed up."

"That's ridiculous!" Sheila shouted.

"Is it?" Max continued. "Did you just make up the story about someone running away from the crime scene? You even had the audacity to say he looked like the other guy that tried to frame you and you claim that there's some video of that guy out of the prison threatening to kill anybody who testifies against him. Is it not enough that he's locked up for one murder? Since he tried to frame you are you trying to frame him, too?"

Chief Anderson folded his sheet of paper and started to put it back in his pocket but gave up. It was too soggy and was falling apart.

"Mr. Sharp, why don't you go get yourself some lunch and we can talk later. Mrs. Mason, could you step into the office for a moment? I have a few questions."

Sheila threw her arms up in disbelief then begrudgingly stepped into the office. As soon as Chief Anderson turned his back I rushed out from under the desk and tried to sneak in. The office door slammed in my face.

Max couldn't hide a big smirk as he made his way to the elevator and pushed the call button which was working properly now and dinged immediately, thanks to Jimmy.

"Forget about changing sheets. Get down here now, Julia!"

Tarrie Ann disconnected her call with Julia and dialed Becky.

"Is Evelyn okay? Good. Let her sleep and come to the lobby ASAP. Chief Anderson is questioning Sheila now. He thinks she might have killed Kevin!"

Officer Reid and Kojak reappeared in the hallway so I slunk back under the front desk. Seeing the office door closed, Officer Reid reconnected Kojak's lead and left the building with a quick nod to Tarrie Ann who pretended to still be on the phone.

The elevator dinged again. Julia stepped out in her neon workout clothes and latex gloves, wiping sweat from her forehead. The coast was clear now so I moved out from under the desk and returned to the comfy chair by the plastic palm tree.

Julia walked slowly to the front desk. "These writers sure know how to mess up a hotel room in a hurry."

Tarrie Ann spoke in a tense but quiet voice. "Forget about that. Chief Anderson's gone from thinking Kevin's death was an accident to blaming Sheila for it! He's questioning her right now." She pointed at the closed office door.

"You can't be serious!" Julia answered loudly.

Tarrie Ann put a finger to her lips and furrowed her brow.

"Becky's on her way. We've got to figure out what really happened before he finally pins one on her. Have you seen Victor Bloodworth? The older man in the fishing cap who always has a crowd around him?"

Julia nodded. "He was in his room, resting in a chair, when I went to clean it. Told me he didn't need anything."

"He seems nice. Maybe too nice. And he has a habit of disappearing right before anything happens. He left the last session as it was starting then somebody put a pair of golf gloves on top of the chief's notebook. And Sheila said he left the bar last night a few minutes before she found Kevin's body. Is he still in his room?"

"I think I heard him leave just before the others came out from their last session. He probably went out for lunch."

"That doesn't leave a lot of options here in Paradise Cove. Frank's Fish Tales is the only place to get a full lunch."

Julia pulled at the latex glove on her right hand.

"I could use a bite. I'll go and see if I can overhear anything."

Tarrie Ann lowered her eyebrows and looked Julia up and down.

"In that outfit?"

Julia looked down at herself and gave Tarrie Ann a "What do you mean?" look.

The elevator door dinged open again and Becky stepped out, her stiletto heels stabbing the carpet with each step. Her black suit looked as though she had ironed it before coming down from Evelyn's private apartment on the top floor.

"Hungry?" Tarrie Ann asked as she walked up to the desk.

Eleven

Frank's Fish Tales was packed. Most of the conference attendees were there, enjoying loud conversations at several tables. One table, though, was relatively quiet with seven diners attentively listening to one man. Victor Bloodworth.

Frank had made it clear on a previous visit that his restaurant was one of the few places in Paradise Cove that wasn't pet-friendly. He didn't trust cats near all of his fresh seafood. I understood that, but on this occasion, I needed to be in there. There was no time to waste if Sheila was a suspect again. Fortunately, there was room for me to move between the tables and the wall so I could stay hidden. I crept inside a lobster cage Frank had set out to create some ambiance. Becky took a seat at the bar not far from Victor's table.

"It is good that we do not have to try to kill the sun or the moon or the stars. It is enough to live on the sea and kill our true brothers."

Victor looked around the table at his captivated audience.

"Anyone?"

One of the men spoke up. "Melville. Moby Dick."

Victor shook his head and laughed. "Nice try." He removed his cap and waved it around. "Anybody else? Nobody recognizes that line?"

None of the others ventured a guess.

"Papa. Ernest Hemingway. From The Old Man and the Sea. The proprietor here has certainly killed some fine fish, or at least he has a good supplier who does. Everyone enjoy your lunch?"

The men and women at the table all agreed and raised their glasses in a toast to the fishermen.

A bell on the restaurant door announced someone coming or going. I turned and saw Officer Reid entering. Kojak stood guard outside the door, respecting the no-pets policy even though he wasn't actually a pet but a working police officer.

Officer Reid scanned the room until he spotted Victor. He walked over to the table and pulled a plastic bag from his pocket. It contained a USB drive that looked like the one found at the crime scene.

"Mr. Bloodworth, is this the item that was taken from your hotel room?"

Victor squinted then nodded. He reached for the bag but Officer Reid pulled it away.

"I'm afraid this is evidence and we can't return it to you at the moment. We do have a few questions, though. Would you be able to join me at the police station?"

"Now?"

Officer Reid looked down at Victor's empty plate.

"It looks like you've finished your lunch and it might help us wrap up the investigation quickly."

The restaurant had gotten quiet and all eyes were on Victor.

"Officer, am I suspect in this man's murder?"

"We're just trying to assemble all the facts at the moment. We haven't even determined for certain that a crime has been committed. Other than theft, if this is indeed your property. It was found in the pocket of the drowning victim. There's a file on here with the name Mr. Eugene ... "

"I'll be happy to come with you," Victor interrupted. He stood quickly, pulling out his wallet and handing some cash to one of the other diners. "Would you please settle my bill for me?"

They walked out together and I followed, waiting until the door had almost closed before darting out once Kojak moved away. Sometimes Officer Reid allowed Kojak to ride in the passenger seat of his truck but with Victor riding up front Kojak was placed in his cage behind the cab. I hopped into the truck bed as the engine started.

"I thought I smelled you," Kojak growled. "You're a brave cat coming anywhere near us after that stunt you pulled with the chief."

"It was funny though, wasn't it?"

Kojak tried not to laugh but he couldn't help himself. "You should've seen Officer Reid. As soon as we got out of the lobby he lost it. I thought he was going to pee in his own pants!"

We shared a laugh for a moment then I got serious again. "Chief Anderson is questioning Sheila now. He thinks she might have killed Kevin. What's on the USB drive that they want to question Victor about?"

"We plugged it in as soon as it dried out and found a password-protected file. It's the only thing on the drive and the file name is Mr. Eugene Black. Officer Reid did some checking and Eugene Black is Victor Bloodworth's real name. He writes under a fake name and seems to have worked hard to hide his true identity."

I recalled the conversation in the lobby where Victor told Max and Isabella about his first book. He told them he changed his name after that and seemed very determined to not let people find out. He had offered £50,000 if anyone had a copy of the book so that he could burn it. Was it just badly written or was there something in it that he wanted to keep hidden? How far might he go to keep his secret?

Kojak was sharing with me so it was only fair that I share something with him. "The ladies noticed that he was nowhere to be seen when Kevin was killed and then again when the gloves were placed on top of Chief Anderson's notebook. He disappeared just before both of those things happened."

"What gloves?"

Kojak didn't know about the gloves. He had left, pretending to search for me, right before the chief discovered them. I filled him in.

"So you think Victor's our guy?"

I thought about it for a second. "He's hiding something, and I think it's more than his name. But did he kill Kevin? I don't know."

We were passing the Parrot Eyes Inn so when the truck stopped for the stop sign I said goodbye and hopped out. Kojak promised to let me know if he found out anything more.

Finding the hotel door closed, I sought out a shady spot on the sidewalk and curled up for a quick catnap. It had been a long day already and it was only lunchtime.

My mind was busy as I tried to rest. I thought about all of the suspects, going over means, motive, and opportunity.

I had to agree with Sheila that the man who ran past us looked somewhat like Roger, at least from behind. And killing Kevin would get rid of one of the witnesses in his upcoming trial. But there were other witnesses and he was locked up in Miami. Despite what Kevin said, I didn't believe he could sneak out.

Victor had a motive. Kevin had stolen from him and may have uncovered whatever secret Victor was hiding. Opportunity? He left the bar just before Sheila was supposed to meet Kevin so he could have gone out to the pool and surprised him. He was the only conference attendee who wasn't in Max's session when Sheila was away from the front desk. Means. Was Victor strong enough to swing a large umbrella and knock Kevin unconscious into the pool? I wasn't sure that he was.

Max was strong enough. I didn't know where he was during Kevin's murder. Was jealousy over a girl he didn't even have a relationship with a strong enough motive to kill?

What about Isabella? She claimed that Buffy made up the rumors about her stealing the story for her best-selling novel. But if the rumors were true, could she have paid Kevin to steal a story from Victor's room and then killed him to tie up loose ends? It was easy to imagine that she had noticed his ankle monitor and decided he was someone who could be bought or blackmailed.

But how would Isabella have placed the gloves on Chief Anderson's notebook? And why? Those gloves didn't make any sense.

The whole hotel was full of possible suspects. I had to narrow it down soon before Chief Anderson narrowed his list down to just Sheila.

I had just managed to fall asleep when a large vehicle pulled up in front of the Inn. It was a van with a satellite dish antenna mounted on top and a News 5 Miami logo on the side. A skinny woman with long blonde hair stepped out of the passenger side holding a microphone.

"Hurry up, Danny! I want to get some interviews before the other stations get here!"

TWELVE

"Are you rolling?"

"I'm rolling."

"Let's go!"

The blonde reporter and Danny, her cameraman, burst in the front door of the Parrot Eyes Inn and rushed straight to the reception desk. I stepped in behind them. Julia and Tarrie Ann looked up from behind the desk with startled looks on their faces.

"Pamela Prince, News 5 Miami. I'm looking for any witnesses to the murder that took place here last night."

Julia screamed and ducked under the desk. Danny pointed his camera at Tarrie Ann. Pamela stuck out her microphone.

"What can you tell us about the man who was found floating in the hotel pool?"

Tarrie Ann adjusted her hair.

Danny moved his face away from the camera viewfinder and then back again. Then he leaned over and whispered in the reporter's ear.

Pamela gave Danny a questioning look and he nodded. She turned back to Tarrie Ann and pulled the microphone to her own face. "We're speaking with Tarrie Ann Thomas, famous for her role on the TV show ... "

Just then the office door burst open and Chief Anderson barged out.

"What's goin' on out ... "

He stopped dead in his tracks as soon as he saw the television camera.

Pamela saw the police logo and 'Chief Anderson' embroidered on the front of his polo shirt. She jerked Danny's camera away from a disappointed Tarrie Ann and pointed it at the chief.

"Chief Anderson. Is it true that the fingerprints on your murder weapon match those of Roger Cabot, a man who is already in prison for another murder? How do you explain that?"

The chief looked confused. "I don't know whose fingerprints are on the murder weapon if it was an actual murder weapon. We haven't gotten results back yet from the forensics lab."

He reached into his pocket and pulled out his cell phone, seemingly looking for any messages he might have missed. The camera was still pointed at him when all the color drained from his face.

"Chief Anderson? What can you tell us?"

"Ahem. Uh. I don't know how you got that information so quickly but, yes, the forensics lab has identified fingerprints on the umbrella found at the crime scene. They are a match to ... Roger Cabot."

"And that's the same man who is in prison right now awaiting trial for another murder here in Paradise Cove. Is that correct?"

Chief Anderson nodded with a confused look on his face.

"And why did you recently check out evidence related to Mr. Cabot's case?"

"Evidence? What are you talking about?"

"We got an anonymous tip that you checked out the gloves with the victim's blood, the only physical evidence tying Roger Cabot to the murder."

Chief Anderson's eyes bulged and a vein on his neck was throbbing. "I did not check them out!"

"According to the evidence log, you did. Here, see for yourself." The reporter showed Chief Anderson her phone.

Sheila stepped out of the office, looking to see what was going on. The chief motioned for her to go back.

"Just wait for me in the office, please, Mrs. Mason."

"Mrs. Mason? *Sheila* Mason?"

Danny pointed the camera at Sheila and Pamela approached her, pointing the microphone toward her face.

"Please tell us what you saw last night. Is it true that you saw Roger Cabot running away from the dead body?"

"I, uh. It *looked* like Roger. I don't know."

Chief Anderson shoved his open palm in front of the camera lens.

"That's enough! Put that camera down! Mrs. Mason, please, go back inside the office and close the door."

Several of the conference attendees had returned from lunch and were standing just inside the front door watching. Becky walked in through them, quickly assessed the situation, and took charge.

"This hotel is private property and unless you have a reservation I'm going to have to insist that you leave the premises."

"We'd like to reserve two rooms," Pamela countered.

"I'm sorry. We're fully booked for a conference. Now, take your camera and leave the premises immediately."

Pamela glared at her but headed out the door, Danny getting video of the onlookers as he followed behind.

Immediately the writers began chattering amongst themselves.

"This is like one of our novels. The evidence says the crime was committed by someone who couldn't possibly have done it."

"Has the police chief been messing with evidence?"

"What does it have to do with Victor? Why was he taken in for questioning?"

"And why did the victim have Victor's USB drive?"

"Look, there's another TV truck. I'm going to see if they want an interview. This might help me sell some books!"

I hoped Evelyn was still asleep upstairs. Her hotel had become a three-ring circus and her son's death was the main attraction. It might be more than she could handle.

Chief Anderson was ushering Sheila back into the office. I took a gamble and snuck in before the door closed. There were several boxes in a corner and I settled in between them to listen.

"Do you believe me now?" Sheila asked.

"It can't be Roger. No way."

"You said it yourself. The umbrella used to kill Kevin had Roger's fingerprints on it. And those gloves somebody left for you … they look like Roger's gloves, like the ones hanging from the man's pocket when he ran past me at the pool. If they are Roger's gloves you won't be able to use them as evidence anymore because they've been tainted. They've got your fingerprints on them now. And mine! Kevin said Roger threatened to kill him. It looks like he kept his promise."

"Roger's in prison. I called this morning and had them send me all of his records. Locked up tight as a drum."

"So how do you explain it, chief?"

"I can't. Yet. But I will." He stared at the gloves on the desk in front of him. Looking at them now I could see some dark stains on them, possibly blood.

Sheila stood up to leave. "Let me know when you figure it out."

"I'm not finished with you yet, Mrs. Mason."

"Unless you're arresting me, yes you are. I've got a hotel to run while my friend Evelyn grieves for her son. Keeping it going is the least I can do for her.

What you need to do is find his killer, and it's not me!"

Sheila walked out, leaving Chief Anderson speechless.

Evelyn, dressed in a house robe with her hair a mess, walked in as soon as Sheila left.

"Your permission to use my office has been rescinded. Please remove yourself from my hotel." She sniffed, looked at the chief's leather chair, and added "And take your stinky chair with you."

I didn't want to be trapped in a room with Chief Anderson so I jumped out from behind the boxes and out the door. Sheila, Becky, Tarrie Ann, and Julia were huddled around Evelyn behind the reception desk explaining what had happened.

I needed a chance to think about these latest developments. It was strange enough that Roger's fingerprints were on the umbrella but what really worried me was how did the news crew know about it? They had to drive all the way here from Miami so they were tipped off hours before the chief got the email. Was their source the same person who told them the gloves were missing? Chief Anderson said he didn't check them out of evidence but now he had possession of them so was he lying? Did he make up the story about them appearing on the desk while he was gone?

Normally I would have enjoyed watching Chief Anderson struggling to get his big chair out of Evelyn's office, then struggling again to get it through the front doors while television cameras captured his frustration. But this case kept getting stranger and I had a very bad feeling about what would happen next.

THIRTEEN

Sheila had finally convinced Evelyn to go back up to her suite and rest. At least two more news trucks had arrived and reporters were taking turns interviewing the writers who were all eager to get a little free publicity. I crept outside and listened to a few of them. I'll give them credit for one thing. They were creative. They loved telling stories.

"I saw the mystery man running away from the pool last night. He leaped over the fence like it was only two feet high. We're probably talking about a professional athlete. There are several professional teams in Florida. The killer might be a celebrity!"

"Don't you find it odd that this Roger fellow is being accused again by the same woman? A woman who was the original suspect in the first murder and just happened to discover the body and is pointing a finger at the same man again, even though he's locked up? I bet they had some relationship and he broke it off. She's a woman scorned, I'm telling you."

"I'm told that this charming little village had never had a murder until this witness showed up. Now this is the fourth one in a year. She moved in and started a club called the Paradise Cove Murder Society. Maybe they're not *solving* murders. Maybe they're *committing* murders!"

One man waited at least twenty minutes for a reporter to notice him then, as soon as the camera was rolling, told them "I'm sorry, I can't speak to you. The police have asked me to consult on the case because of my extensive history in creating elaborate murder plots in my best-selling novels which you can find in the mystery section of your local bookstore." He started to walk away then stepped back in front of the camera. "Iain Chesterton. That's Iain with two ... "

The cameraman pointed his camera away before the writer could finish.

I'd heard enough to know that the writers had plenty of fantastical ideas but they didn't have a clue. I waited until one woman finished her interview then followed her through the door back into the hotel lobby. Sheila had returned from Evelyn's suite and was back behind the reception desk. Julia was carrying some cleaning supplies to the elevator. Becky was heading out to meet a potential client. Tarrie Ann was nowhere to be seen. I jumped up into my new favorite chair beside the palm tree.

"Call me if you need me," Becky said as she headed to the back door, away from the reporters out front.

The phone at the desk rang.

"It's a beautiful day at the Parrot Eyes Hotel. How may I help you?"

Sheila listened for a moment.

"Of course, Mr. Bloodworth. I'll take care of it."

She hung up the phone.

Jimmy was coming down the hallway carrying a bucket of paint and a large brush. Sheila motioned to him.

"Would you mind opening up room 113 when Officer Reid gets here? He needs to retrieve something." Sheila held out a keycard which Jimmy attempted to take with his left hand and dropped the brush. A streak of blue paint added a little extra color to the 1980s-looking carpet. I doubted anyone would ever notice.

"I'll hold on to those for you," Sheila offered, taking the paint supplies and setting them behind the desk.

The noise outside picked up and I saw Officer Reid pushing his way through the reporters. He stepped inside and quickly pushed the door closed.

"I've been asked to ... "

"Follow me," Jimmy interrupted. He waved the keycard and motioned for the officer to follow him.

I had hoped Kojak would be along. We already had plenty of new developments to discuss but he was either back at the station or in the truck.

Jimmy and Officer Reid were only gone about a minute before they reappeared in the hallway, walking our way. I looked to see what they had taken from Victor's room but didn't see anything. Officer Reid had his left hand in his pocket and my sensitive cat ears did pick up a slight rattle as he passed me on his way out. Keys? No, I didn't think that was it but I couldn't quite place it.

"What did he take?" Sheila asked as soon as the door closed.

"Dunno. He just walked into the bathroom and came right back out. It looked like he was putting something in his pocket but I couldn't see what it was."

"Victor's been talking to the police for quite a while. Becky said they took him from the restaurant and had recovered his property from Kevin. It was the USB drive and there was a file they seemed interested in. It had a name, Eugene some-body, but she didn't hear the last name."

She didn't hear it because Officer Reid didn't say it. Victor, who was one of the most polite people I'd ever met, had interrupted him as soon as he started to say the name. I hadn't thought about it at the time but now it struck me as odd. Out of character, at least.

Jimmy was frowning.

"Sheila, don't you think this murder society business is a bit much? I know the police department hasn't exactly earned a lot of confidence but maybe you should focus on the hotel and Evelyn. Let them handle the investigation."

Jimmy had been busy with the repairs and hadn't been brought up to speed. Sheila filled him in and he wasn't happy with what she told him.

"Forget what I said about letting the police do their jobs. We need to figure out what's going on before they go down the wrong path again! This Victor Bloodworth must be involved. There's no telling what stories he's spinning for Chief Anderson. The guy is a master storyteller."

Sheila defended Victor. "He seems so nice. And I just know that Roger is behind it all."

"That's what somebody *wants* you to think," Jimmy said.

That was a good point. I couldn't believe that Roger had somehow escaped from prison and killed Kevin but somehow the evidence pointed at him. His fingerprints were on the murder weapon. Did somebody else put them there? If so, how did they get them? From the gloves? That would be tricky, if not impossible. And that's if they were Roger's gloves. I was inclined to believe now that they were.

A shout from down the hall got our attention. It was Tarrie Ann standing just outside the open door to the bar.

"You need to come see this!"

Jimmy, Sheila, and I quickly made our way to the bar where Tarrie Ann had apparently been hiding out. A half-empty margarita glass sat on a table and the television on the wall was on. The front of the Parrot Eyes Inn was on the screen as Pamela Prince gave a live report.

"Police have not identified a suspect in the case but what we do know is that the evidence, a fingerprint on the murder weapon, points to a man who was in a Miami prison when the crime occurred. Roger Cabot's attorney released a statement moments ago."

Julia rushed in as a middle-aged man in an expensive suit appeared on screen.

"We just discovered that the only physical evidence that supposedly linked my client to the murder he has already been falsely accused of has gone missing, taken from a secure facility by the investigating police chief, and not returned. Is this because it would have exonerated my client? Now the primary witness, the man who prosecutors built their case around, has died and can no longer be questioned about his involvement in the crime or about the deal he made to get himself released while my client remained behind bars. This is unfair and unequal treatment. I have submitted paperwork demanding that the court release Roger Cabot due to lack of evidence. I am further demanding an inquiry into the actions of the Paradise Cove police department as well as a group of women who call themselves the Paradise Cove Murder Society and may well be responsible for multiple murders in that town."

A gasp went up from Sheila, Julia, and Tarrie Ann. Jimmy was silent.

Tarrie Ann gulped down the rest of her margarita. "I'll make us all a pitcher."

Pamela Prince was back on screen.

"While Roger Cabot's attorney works to get him out of prison, the woman who discovered the body here at the Parrot Eyes Inn last night claims she saw the incarcerated man at the crime scene."

The image on the screen switched to a close-up of Sheila from when the reporter ambushed her earlier.

"It *looked* like Roger."

"Sheila Mason is reputed to be the leader of the Paradise Cove Murder Society. There's so much more we're learning about the murders in this quiet seaside village. I'm Pamela Prince. Stay tuned to News 5 Miami."

As a pair of news anchors in the studio took over, the text at the bottom of the screen read "Who Framed Roger Cabot?"

FOURTEEN

I paced the floor in the lobby while Sheila busied herself behind the reception desk. Tarrie Ann had eventually come out of the bar and stood behind the desk watching the news on her phone. Julia had gone back to clean more rooms and Jimmy had taken his painting supplies upstairs. None of them had come up with any ideas to keep Roger from getting released and the hotel wouldn't wait. There was another day before the conference ended.

Isabella walked through the lobby and out the front door, looking very professional in a business suit and heels. This morning she had been wearing jeans and sneakers but had apparently gone to her room to change before granting interviews to the reporters who remained on the sidewalk. She gave a disgusted look as Max walked in past her with a book in his hand and a huge smile on his face.

Tarrie Ann looked up from her phone.

"Oh, is that the book you promised to sign for me?"

She reached out but Max pulled the book away. His smile disappeared. "No," was all he said as he walked over to the elevator and pressed the call button.

The front door opened again and shouts from outside streamed in.

"Mr. Bloodworth! Will you comment on the murder here at the hotel?"

Victor deftly sidestepped the reporters and moved inside quickly, looking much more spry than he had earlier. I began to rethink the possibility that he could have been the mystery man who jumped over the pool gate. Victor took a deep breath to collect himself, smiled and nodded toward Sheila and Tarrie Ann, then walked briskly toward the hallway, past the elevator where Max was repeatedly pressing the call button. It looked like Jimmy would have to work on it some more.

When Max noticed Victor he called out to him and smiled again. It was an even bigger smile than before. Max looked like the fabled 'cat that ate the canary,' although I've always despised that expression. Cats don't smile like humans. We generally don't smile at all. When we do, we smile with our eyes but that's beside the point. Max was grinning from ear to ear as he showed Victor the book he was carrying. Victor reached out but, just as he had done with Tarrie Ann, Max pulled the book away. He made such a show of it that Sheila and Tarrie Ann started watching. The men lowered their voices.

Victor reached into his coat pocket and pulled out a checkbook and pen. He was an old-fashioned man. He opened the checkbook and started to write in it before Max shook his head. Victor appeared upset and reached for the book again with no success. Frustrated, he strode quickly down the hallway toward his room.

The elevator finally dinged and Buffy walked out as the doors opened. Max stepped inside and disappeared. Buffy checked her hair in a mirror on the wall and made her way to the reporters outside.

"What do you suppose is so important about the book Max was carrying?" Sheila asked Tarrie Ann.

"I have no idea. I've never heard of the author. It said Eugene Black. The title was under his hand so I couldn't see that."

I recognized that name. Kojak had said it when we were talking in the back of the truck earlier. Eugene Black was Victor's real name and the name of the file on the USB drive Kevin had stolen from him. Victor had told Max and Isabella that he would pay £50,000 for any copy of his first book so that he could destroy it. It was so embarrassing, he said, that he changed his name. Max must have found a copy at the used bookstore in town, Guilty Pleasures and Dusty Treasures. The store name was appropriate because half the books in there hadn't been taken off the shelf in decades.

What didn't make sense was that Victor had been ready to pay up and Max refused to sell. Surely he didn't think anyone else would pay more than £50,000 for a used book that had been passed over by every visitor to the bookstore for years?

Victor's secrets were getting more and more interesting. What was on the password-protected file on the USB drive? Was there something in the book that was more than embarrassing? Why did he keep disappearing and had he been pretending to be slow and frail with age?

Becky appeared in the hallway, coming from the back door.

"Have you seen the news?" she said as soon as she was close enough to be heard without yelling.

Sheila and Tarrie Ann nodded grimly.

"So much for getting a little real estate work done. We have to figure this out before it's too late."

"Where do you suggest we start?" Sheila asked. "We're all out of ideas. I'd love to confront Roger and find out what he's up to but, as everybody keeps pointing out, he's in prison in Miami."

Becky shook her head. "Roger's gotten into your head, Sheila. He's just trying to exploit the situation. We have to focus on the people who were here last night and figure out if any of them had a reason to kill Kevin. Most of the attendees were in the bar with you last night, weren't they? Did you go anywhere between the time you left the bar and when you got to the pool?"

Sheila thought for a second.

"No. I stepped out of the bar, waited in the hall for just a minute getting up my nerve, and then went out to the pool. If anyone had left the bar I would have seen them."

"Did anybody come into the bar just before you left? Close enough that they could have done it?"

"Not that I noticed. Well, Evelyn. But you don't think she ... "

Becky and Tarrie Ann glanced at each other in awkward silence. The elevator door dinged, breaking the tension, and Julia stepped out pushing a cart full of sheets that needed to be washed.

"You're all having a murder society meeting while I change bedsheets? I think it's time we switched jobs for a while!"

"We were just wondering ... " Becky looked around and lowered her voice. "Is there any chance that Evelyn ... "

Julia looked confused for a moment then her mouth dropped and her eyes bulged.

"No! I mean, she had to be frustrated taking care of her adult son at this age after he conspired with a murderer to take over her business, but ... well, when I put it that way ... "

Sheila wouldn't hear it. "Absolutely not. Evelyn is heartbroken. She loved Kevin, no matter what he did or tried to do."

"Ok," Becky leaned over the reception desk and rested her head on her hands. "That brings us back to the one person we know *left* the bar right before you did. Victor. He couldn't have been far away."

"But not everybody was in the bar," Sheila said. "I didn't see Max or Isabella there. Isabella says she took a walk on the beach but there are no witnesses. We don't know where Max was."

Tarrie Ann jumped in. "We don't know where they were last night but they were both in the conference room when Victor left and you came in to check on Whiskers. Max was leading the session and I was sitting next to Isabella. How would either of them have put the gloves on Evelyn's desk?"

Becky stood up straight again and looked determined. "Victor had the opportunity both times. And Kevin had stolen his USB drive with a password-protected file on it. So we're back to where we were before the media circus started. When Officer Reid came into the restaurant with the USB drive he didn't seem too excited but as soon as Officer Reid started to say the name of the file, Victor jumped up and went with him. He was at the police station for quite a while. I'd love to know what they talked about. He has to be … "

Sheila put a finger to her lips and Becky stopped talking.

"Don't let me interrupt you ladies," Victor said in his charming English accent as he walked into the lobby. He pushed open the front door and called out to the writers outside. "My most sincere apologies for the delay. I'm ready to get started on my next presentation now if you've all had your five minutes of fame."

Victor held the door open as the conference attendees walked back in and headed to the conference room.

When all the writers had gone in for the session and closed the door Becky started walking to the hotel entrance. "Let's find out what the police asked him."

"You're just going to walk into the police station and ask Chief Anderson to tell you?" Sheila asked.

"Not by myself. There are several people on the sidewalk who are very good at asking questions. Maybe they can demand some answers once I tell them what we know."

FIFTEEN

I hopped down from my seat and followed Becky out of the hotel's main entrance. The reporters and cameramen had gone back to their separate news trucks but came running when they realized Becky a member of the Paradise Cove Murder Society was outside.

Pamela Prince was the first to thrust a microphone in Becky's face.

"Roger Cabot has accused the Paradise Cove Murder Society of being a group of murderers. What is your response?"

Becky didn't respond to the question. She addressed all of the reporters at once.

"While you were all out here talking to people who don't have a clue what happened, the police were busy talking to a man who might be the killer. Victor Bloodworth, one of the few writers at this conference who hasn't given you an interview, had complained about the victim just hours before the murder, saying Kevin stole something from his room. Our investigation has revealed that Mr. Bloodworth had the motive, means, and opportunity to commit the crime. If you want a scoop for your next newscast, I suggest you drive down to the police station and demand that Chief Anderson tell you what was on the USB drive stolen from Mr. Bloodworth and found on the victim's dead body. You should also ask him what his officer retrieved from Mr. Bloodworth's room while they were interviewing him at the station."

Cameramen immediately started packing up their cameras and tripods as quickly as they could and getting back in their vans. The police station was just a few blocks away so I took off down the sidewalk and arrived at the same time as the News 5 Miami van. Officer Reid was just leaving with Kojak in the passenger seat of his truck.

Pamela Prince stepped out of her van, followed by Becky who had gotten a ride. The cameraman,

Danny got out of the driver's side door and went to the back to retrieve his equipment. Three more news vehicles pulled in moments later, filling the small parking lot, and soon the tiny lobby of the building was overflowing with reporters demanding to speak to the chief. The room was only about eight feet wide with a door and a thick window that had a small opening to pass papers through.

My tail got stepped on several times despite my best efforts to avoid feet in the crowded lobby. I managed to hop up onto the counter briefly before being shoved off when a cameraman set his gear down. There was a small table between the counter and the locked door going into the main office so I curled up underneath it.

During my brief time on the counter, I spotted Chief Anderson standing behind his chairless desk with his office door wide open.

"Officer Reid!" The chief called out, hoping someone else could deal with the media but no one else was in the office. He sighed and moaned as he made his way to the lobby and pushed the security door open, forcing reporters and cameramen to squeeze even closer together.

"We're gonna hafta take this outside," the chief said loudly over the noise of the mob.

The outside door opened and I had to make a choice. I could step out with the reporters and hear what Chief Anderson told them or I could try to sneak into the empty office and take a look at whatever was on the chief's desk. A lesson from my mentor, Fred, came to mind. He had told me never to worry about attending press conferences. If the police said anything important you would hear it later on TV. My better option was to go inside, look around for any information he wasn't sharing with the public, and hope I would be able to get out before he spotted me.

As soon as the lobby started to clear, but before Chief Anderson followed the press members, I snuck around his legs and into the inner office. Hopping onto the desk on the other side of the lobby window, I watched Chief Anderson escort the press members outside, along with Becky who looked back and spotted me inside. Her eyes went wide for a brief moment before she hid her surprise to keep the chief from looking. The outside door closed and I was alone.

For a moment I just stood there, soaking in the office. I was an intruder, but I didn't feel that way. Over the last few months, I'd helped solve three murders in Paradise Cove, sharing information from my investigations with Kojak. Not all of my information, but enough to feel like I was part of the team. The badge I wore on my collar had been given to me in Colorado so, regardless of how genuine anyone considered it to be, I was way out of my jurisdiction. Maybe one day Chief Anderson would recognize my efforts and skills and give me an official role in the department. Then again, after what I'd done to his beloved chair, probably not.

I shook myself out of my daze and got to work. Hopping down from the front desk, I padded my way into the chief's private office and jumped up to explore his desk. It was covered in papers, everything from handwritten notes to a brochure for a new fishing boat. The computer screen was on and I caught just a quick glimpse of an opened email before the screensaver came on, showing images of the chief holding up various fish he had caught. In every picture he held his arm out straight toward the camera, making the fish look larger. I tried to visualize the email I had seen. The subject line said 'DNA results' but I hadn't been able to read the contents quickly enough.

I looked back down at the papers on the desk and spotted the lab report showing that Roger's fingerprints were on the pool umbrella that had been used to knock Kevin into the water. No other fingerprints were found. There were notes from the interviews with potential suspects or witnesses. Buffy had told the chief that Isabella was the likeliest suspect, repeating her claim that Isabella had stolen the story for her best-selling novel and was probably using Kevin to steal a story from Victor.

Isabella denied that she had ever stolen anything but she had told the chief something she had not admitted to us. According to her, Kevin had heard the rumors Buffy was spreading and saw an opportunity. He had taken the USB drive from Victor's room and tried to sell it to her when he went to fix her air conditioner. She claimed to have turned him down and thought about going to the police but decided it would only make Buffy's rumors about her spread faster.

There was a sheet with Max's name at the top but no notes underneath. The chief still hadn't questioned him because he'd interrogated Sheila instead.

I looked around the desk for Chief Anderson's notes about Victor. What was it that Officer Reid had retrieved from Victor's hotel room and why had they kept him at the station so long? There must have been plenty of notes somewhere but I couldn't find them.

What I did discover was unexpected. A printout of an email from a corrections department official to Officer Reid showing Roger's prison record. It showed all the details of his time behind bars including when he arrived, times he had left for court appearances, who had visited him, etc. I wished I had time to look at it more closely but, knowing Chief Anderson as I did, the amount of time he would spend with the press would not be generous. I had to hurry.

As a dedicated officer of the law, it would go against my nature to steal or destroy evidence. The handwritten notes were important and couldn't be replaced. But the email with Roger's prison records could be printed out again or viewed electronically. I began thinking about how I could take it with me. Sneaking back out would be hard enough as it was. I'd surely be spotted carrying papers in my mouth.

Something creaked and caught my attention. I looked out the window to the lobby and the front door to see if the chief was coming back in yet but the door remained closed. As I looked that way I noticed the small opening in the window where visitors could pass papers in or receive them from someone inside. It would be risky but I doubted the chief paid much attention to the window and the counter below it, especially after talking to a crowd of reporters.

Moving quickly in case he or Officer Reid returned, I picked up the printed-out email in my mouth and carried it to the front desk. Using my front paw, I pushed it through the slot in the window until it sat on the counter in the lobby. At this point, I was a little jealous of my friend Roddy who could have easily squeezed himself through the small opening. I would never make it and, if I got stuck trying, the chief would see me and punish me for what I did in his chair.

I positioned myself against the wall beside the door frame and waited. As expected, the wait was short. The front door opened and I heard reporters shouting questions as the chief ignored them and stepped quickly to the security door. A buzzing noise indicated that his access card had worked and, as soon as the door swung open, I swept past his feet back to the lobby.

I had escaped the office and was safe for the moment but trapped in the lobby. Not knowing who would enter next from either door, I curled up again under the small table. A few moments later the front door opened. My view was limited without stepping out from under the table but I could see legs and feet and I would have recognized those high heels anywhere. Becky remembered seeing me inside and had come to my rescue.

I stepped out from under the table and silently rubbed against Becky's ankle, which was about head high thanks to her stiletto heels. She reached down to pick me up but I darted away, hopped up to the counter, and knocked the printout to the floor with a quiet "meow."

"What have you knocked over, Whiskers?"

Becky reached down and picked up the paper, reading enough to realize what I'd delivered to her. Without another word, she collected me in her right arm, carried the paper in her left, and we disappeared unnoticed out the door.

Sixteen

"Detective Whiskers has earned his badge today!"

Becky walked through the front door of the Parrot Eyes Inn proudly waving the printed-out email showing Roger's prison records. She looked around quickly to make sure there were no hotel guests in view then walked over to where Sheila, Julia, Tarrie Ann, and Jimmy were huddled at the reception desk.

I strutted casually to my new favorite chair beside the fake palm tree and hopped up, making sure to shake my head enough to cause a jingle from the badge on my collar.

Nobody looked up. Becky barged into the huddle indignantly.

"What are you all looking at?"

Tarrie Ann held up a paperback book and read aloud from it.

"Police Detective Anita Mann reached out and grabbed the front of her partner's crisply starched uniform shirt, careful not to break a colorfully painted fingernail. 'You think you're so smart just because you've solved hundreds of cases that were supposed to be unsolvable and won a dozen Detective of the Year awards in just the last decade. Well, you're not smart enough to see when the thing you need the most, the *person* you need the most, is right in front of you.' She released her grip on his now-wrinkled shirt and turned away, tears streaming down her Christie Brinkley face then trickling between her Loni Anderson ... "

Becky snatched the book away from Tarrie Ann and slammed it on the desk. "Enough of that trash. Read this." She held out the printed email message and Julia took it.

"Is this what I think it is?"

Becky nodded and grinned smugly. Now that she had everyone's attention, of course, she didn't bother to give me credit. The others all craned their necks to look.

"According to this, Roger hasn't left the prison at all since his last court appearance over eight weeks ago. There's no way he could have killed Kevin and left his fingerprints on the murder weapon."

Sheila let out a big sigh. "I'm not sure if I'm relieved or frustrated. I just know he's responsible for all this, no matter what that piece of paper says."

Julia read further down the paper. "It also has a list of all of his visitors. Maybe Roger had an accomplice. Hubert Howe visited several times. Who is he?"

Sheila recognized the name and answered with an obvious disdain in her voice. "That's Roger's attorney, the guy we saw on TV earlier."

Julia groaned and then continued. "What about the rest of these? Can we pull up a list of the conference attendees and see if any of them match?"

"On it," Sheila answered. "Read them out to me."

Julia read off the short list of Roger's visitors but none of them matched the names of the hotel guests.

"What about nom de plumes?" Julia asked. "Pen names. Pseudonyms. Fake names," she added when everyone just stared at her. "We know Victor changed his name. Maybe some of the other authors did, too."

Sheila pulled up an internet browser on the hotel computer and started typing names from the registry into a search engine looking for nom de plumes. Several of the guests had Wikipedia pages that mentioned different names but none were on the list of prison visitors.

The mood seemed to drop as everyone realized the prison records probably wouldn't be much help. I felt a little less cheated about Becky not giving me proper credit. Then Tarrie Ann remembered that they hadn't shared their latest news with Becky.

"Oh, Becky, while you were gone we did some snooping. That's why we were reading this book."

Tarrie Ann picked the book back up from the desk and showed Becky the cover which featured a muscular police detective placing handcuffs on a big-busted woman. The title was Busted by the Best and the author was Maximus Sharp.

Becky rolled her eyes. "Max wrote that garbage? Seems about right. Did you steal it from his room?"

"Of course not!" Tarrie Ann acted offended. "Jimmy and I went in to make sure everything was working correctly. He promised to give it to me so when I saw it lying there I decided to save him some trouble. He still needs to sign it for me!"

Tarrie Ann set the book down again. "Julia and Sheila did some snooping, too. They went to Victor's room."

Becky looked expectantly at Sheila and Julia who looked at each other trying to decide who would give her the scoop. Sheila nodded for Julia to do the honors.

"Well, we went in to clean the room but it was immaculate. The bed was made, clothes carefully placed on hangers in the closet. Even the towel he used this morning was neatly folded on the floor of the bathroom."

"So you didn't find anything?" Becky let out a disappointed sigh. "He's got to be involved. Always disappearing when things get interesting. Acting old and frail at times, then maneuvering around young reporters with ease. And so secretive about the USB drive Kevin stole from him."

"We did see one thing that could be of interest. He had all of his toiletries laid out neatly by the sink. There was a pill bottle. Any idea what Sinemet is for?"

"Sinemet?" Becky nodded. "I used to pick up medicines for my Aunt Jenny sometimes. She had Parkinson's disease. That was one of the pills she took."

Becky's face lit up. "That would explain ... a lot!"

Everyone stared at her, waiting for an explanation.

"Aunt Jenny lived a mostly normal life for years after she got the disease. As long as her medicine was working everything was fine. But after a while, the medicine's effects didn't last as long. She could barely move until she got another dose, and she had to wait before she could take it or she would overdose. So she always made sure she was some-where safe before the medicine wore off."

"That's why he always disappears," Sheila said. "He doesn't want people to see him when the medicine isn't working. And Officer Reid had to get him his pill bottle before he came back from the police station. Which explains why he was there so long, waiting for his medicine to work. By the time he got back here, he was fine again."

"Doesn't Parkinson's make you shake all over?" Julia asked. "That actor who has it? He can't seem to keep his body from moving during interviews."

"Yeah, some of that is from too much medicine. And the shaking doesn't affect all patients the same way. Aunt Jenny didn't have much of that."

At that point, the doors to the conference room swung open and writers began to pour out.

"I'd better open the bar," Sheila said, hurrying out from behind the reception desk and across the lobby. I hopped down from my chair to follow her then paused behind the palm tree when I spotted Max walking my way with Buffy.

"You've been grinning all afternoon, Max, what's up?"

Buffy stopped in front of me, spotted the chair, and sat down.

"Just excited about my next book." Max was still smiling like a schoolboy talking to a pretty teacher. "It's coming along better than I ever imagined. I'll be on top of the best-seller list for months with this one!"

Buffy sneezed and pulled a tissue from her purse. "Is that cat in here? I'm allergic to cats."

Max pointed to the chair. "I saw it earlier. Sitting right where you are."

"EWWWWW!" Buffy jumped up and strained to look at the back of her fancy dress. My beautiful tuxedo fur looks dapper on me but she wasn't wearing it nearly as well as I do. "I have to go change!"

She marched across the elevator which had just opened for some other guests. She barged in past a few slower, less pushy people.

Max took the stairs. "I'll help you get out of that dress."

I remembered that I had been on my way to the bar which was now full of guests talking loudly and lined up waiting for Sheila to make them drinks. Somebody yelled out "QUIET!" and most of the voices disappeared as the volume on the television was turned up. Pamela Prince was shown in front of the Paradise Cove Police Station.

"Another shocking development here in the bizarre case of a man found dead in a hotel pool last night. Earlier today we were told that finger-prints on the alleged murder weapon were a match for Roger Cabot who was locked in a prison cell many miles away at the time of the crime. Police Chief Gary Anderson has now confirmed there is even more evidence tying Cabot to the crime scene."

The image on the screen switched to a recorded video of the chief.

"While investigating at the scene last night, we took custody of a coffee cup found not far from the deceased. That coffee cup was tested and the DNA on it is a definitive match for Roger Cabot."

A gasp went up in the room. I looked at Sheila who was leaning on the bar looking weak. Victor quickly stepped around and helped her to a seat at a table by the wall.

Despite her condition, Sheila turned back to watch the television where Hubert Howe, Roger's attorney, was making another statement.

"With this latest development, we are amending our petition to have my client released from custody immediately. The police in Paradise Cove, along with the amateur sleuths who call themselves the Paradise Cove Murder Society, have been working together to frame my client for murder. With their original case falling apart, they are manufacturing the most ridiculous, preposterous, slanderous case ever presented in the state of Florida. And that's a big statement. Roger Cabot did not kill anyone earlier this year. He could not have killed the victim last night. He must be set free without delay!"

Pamela Prince appeared on the screen again.

"The judge presiding over Mr. Cabot's trial has announced that she will issue a determination tomorrow morning at 10 AM. I'm Pamela Prince live for News 5 Miami in Paradise Cove, the new murder capital of Florida."

SEVENTEEN

The bar was packed and everyone wanted to talk about the case. Or cases, I should say. Both Kevin's death and the murder that Roger was awaiting trial for. Would Roger be released? How had his DNA ended up at the crime scene? Is the police department incompetent? Were the ladies of the Paradise Cove Murder Society just a group of bored ladies looking for justice or were they like the firemen who started fires so they could put them out?

I had been shooed away from the bar stool by the wall and walked carefully around the room, keeping my tail curled over my back and trying my best to listen to conversations without getting stepped on. I looked for Victor. Nowhere to be seen. Everyone else seemed to be there and they were so excited that it was hard to hear any individual speak, but I made out a few things here and there.

One young man was telling Max and a few others that he had a cousin who was a prison guard. Not where Roger was locked up, but he thought maybe he could get some inside information anyway. If Roger was willing to share his story for a book, somebody could make a killing writing it. Pun intended. A TV deal seemed likely, as well. Max's big smile never left his face. "Good luck with that!" he said as he patted the young man on the back and walked over to another conversation.

Isabella spotted me watching her and tried to pick me up. "Buffy, your friend is here!"

Buffy looked over, her eyes went wide, and she ran off.

It was all getting a little crazy. So crazy, and loud, that Evelyn showed up in her house robe and fuzzy pink flamingo slippers. She placed two fingers in her mouth and whistled. The talking stopped.

Sheila had recovered, somewhat, and was behind the bar pouring drinks as quickly as she could with some help from Tarrie Ann and Jimmy but Evelyn wasn't going to allow it anymore.

"Party's over! Bar is closed."

Everyone stared at the hotel owner like she was crazy.

Sheila protested. "You can't close it now. It's early and they're in the mood to drink and talk all night. You'll sell enough drinks to pay for a lot of repairs. It's exactly what you needed."

"Is it what *you* need? I don't think so. You need to go home and rest."

Sheila opened her mouth to speak but Evelyn shook her head.

"Sheila, I can't thank you and the others enough. There's no way I could have kept this place open without your help. But it's over. The conference will wrap up tomorrow, they'll all go home, and the Parrot Eyes Inn will close its doors. I just can't do it anymore and you can't do it for me forever."

Conference attendees started filing out, looking for somewhere else to continue speculating on the murders. Someone suggested the pool area where Sheila and I had discovered Kevin's lifeless body less than 24 hours earlier. A large group followed them.

Jimmy started collecting dirty glasses from tables but Evelyn stopped him.

"There's no need for that. This mess isn't going anywhere and nobody will be coming in to see it. You all have been here too long. Go home. And take a bottle with you."

Evelyn held the door and ushered us out, bending down to stroke my back as I rubbed up against one of her flamingos.

"Can we at least ... "

Sheila didn't finish her sentence before Evelyn replied firmly. "Go home."

Tarrie Ann carried a bottle of tequila out to her golf cart and drove off. Jimmy and I joined Sheila at her cart, the back still filled with many of the tools he hadn't gotten around to using yet. I hopped up into her lap and she drove to Jimmy's house. Buster barked from behind the fence. I didn't answer.

"Care to come in for a coffee?" he asked as he pulled supplies off and set them in his driveway.

"Another time. Evelyn was right. I need to rest. You should, too."

Jimmy stood and watched as we rode off toward the beach and Sunset Cottage. The neighborhood was quiet. A cool breeze floated in from the water. A nearly full moon provided enough light that Sheila hadn't bothered turning on her headlights. The whir of the electric motor was drowned out by the sound of nocturnal creatures calling each other. Frogs, crickets, Todd, Margo.

Sheila slammed on the brakes just in time to avoid running over the elderly couple who were lying on a blanket in the street. Margo jumped up, pulling her shirt closed. Todd grabbed the blanket and wine bottle. They ran into their house without saying a word. The door slammed, then reopened, and Margo shouted out "Turn on your headlights, you crazy woman!" The door slammed shut again.

Sheila snorted. At first, she tried to hide it but, realizing there was no one else but me around, she snorted again and broke out into a full belly laugh. For a long moment, we just sat there in the road on the golf cart, Sheila laughing away the tension

CHRIS ABERNATHY

of a very long couple of days. Eventually, her laughter died away and we finished the drive home. It must have felt good to walk inside and plop down on the sofa with a bag of chips, which Sheila did immediately after opening a can of Fancy Feast for me. She didn't even bother to scoop it into a bowl, just laid the can down next to my water.

What a stressful time it had been. Sheila had volunteered to help Evelyn with her conference, expecting it to be tiring but mostly uneventful. A chance to help a friend in need and perhaps meet a few famous authors. And Sheila enjoyed having something to do. Retired life at the beach was good when nobody was getting killed, but I'd noticed Sheila becoming a little restless when we stayed home together. We'd watched Jessica Fletcher, Thomas Magnum, Columbo, and all the other great detectives so many times that even if it was an episode we hadn't seen, which was rare, we always figured out whodunit.

The first sign of trouble at the conference had been when Victor Bloodworth had come to Sheila accusing Kevin of stealing from his room. It had all gone downhill from there. Kevin telling Sheila about Roger's threats, finding Kevin's body and seeing someone who might or might not have been Roger, being told she was crazy, getting interrogated for Kevin's murder and ambushed by the press. Then the possibility that Roger, who was definitely a killer and had very nearly ruined our move to Paradise Cove as soon as we arrived, might be released from prison as soon as tomorrow.

By the time I finished my Fancy Feast, Sheila's head was on the arm of the sofa and she was snoring lightly. The bag of chips was still in her hand, tipped over with several pieces falling onto the floor.

I heard a scratching noise and saw Roddy peek out of his crack in the wall. His eyes locked on the fallen food then he turned to me with a pleading expression.

"Go ahead," I meowed quietly. "Just be quiet," I warned, although I suspected even Buster, Jimmy's rambunctious dog, couldn't have woken Sheila up at this point.

Roddy scampered out and began feasting, nervously glancing up at Sheila's hand which hovered inches above his head. I watched until he had cleaned up all the fallen pieces then scurried back inside the wall to take his own nap.

I needed a nap, too. But I couldn't relax. Could Roger really get released? Would he come back to Paradise Cove if he did? Who killed Kevin? Despite the fingerprint and DNA on the coffee cup, I didn't believe for a minute that Roger had escaped, committed another murder, and then gone back to prison. None of it made sense. Perhaps a walk on the beach would help.

Sheila had uncharacteristically left the pantry door open so I took the opportunity to nab a catnip treat. Not for myself, mind you. I carried the treat through the pet door, down the boardwalk, and into the dunes.

"Whiskers, my man! You're the best!"

Zappa meandered out from around a clump of sea oats.

"I knew I smelled 'nip!"

I laid the treat down for Zappa who dove in with glee. I sat quietly while he enjoyed the treat. When it was gone he looked at me with a contented smile that fell into a concerned frown.

"You look troubled, man. What's stuck in your whiskers, Whiskers?"

"Roger might be coming back."

"Roger? Do I know Roger? Is he a bad dude?"

I stared at Zappa. Sometimes I envied his simple life but I don't think I could ever live as worry-free as he did.

"Roger who killed Mitch and framed Sheila for it. We just talked about it yesterday."

"Oh. Yeah. That dude. That's bad, man. I thought he was locked up."

I couldn't be bothered to explain it all. I'd brought Zappa some catnip and saw that he was fine. Time to move on and take that walk I came outside for.

"Gotta run. I'll explain it later."

"Explain what, man?"

"Never mind."

I walked out of the dunes toward the water's edge and slowly strolled in the direction of the pier. Ghost crabs flitted around, going in and out of their little holes in the white sand. The tide was heading out and I saw Blue's tracks still visible.

She must have been here not long ago. She'd be happy to see Jimmy back tomorrow. With Evelyn calling it quits there was no need for him to go back for more repairs. He could come fishing and toss some fresh seafood to Blue and Zappa again. He'd have Buster with him, of course.

I wished I could talk to Blue about what was happening. She was a great listener. The best. She never argued with me, told me I was crazy, or interrupted with some story of her own that she thought was related even though it wasn't. She just listened. Every once in a while I'd get a little nod, just to let me know she hadn't tuned me out, but that was about it. I loved our talks.

Squatting quietly in the sand, I stared at the moon's reflection on the water and imagined Blue beside me. Still as a statue, she stood tall watching for any movement under the waves while listening to me ramble. What would she say if she truly were here? Nothing. And that's all I needed at the moment. A little bit of nothing to clear my head. Somehow she'd managed to give me exactly what I needed without even being here. Maybe things would make more sense in the morning.

EIGHTEEN

I had expected Sheila to sleep in. She needed the rest but must have decided it could wait. I was surprised to see her stumble into the kitchen rubbing her eyes before seven o'clock.

"Evelyn still needs me, Whiskers. It's the last day of the conference and guests will be needing help at the check-out desk. After today she can close it down if that's what she wants to do, but I'm going to make sure she gets through today alright."

If Sheila was going to be at the hotel, then so was I. I ate my Fancy Feast while she showered then rode in my customary spot on the back of the golf cart. We stopped at Sea Brews for a coffee and all the chatter was about Roger. And the Paradise Cove Murder Society.

"Do you think he was framed?" one woman asked the barista as she accepted her Salty Beaches latte.

"Something's up. He can't have killed both of them so you have to wonder if he killed either of them. It's all a little too perfect, these ladies catching a bunch of ... "

The barista's voice trailed off when she noticed Sheila. The customer looked back and then rushed out with her drink.

Sheila smiled and pretended she hadn't heard anything.

"Good morning, Abby. I'll have my usual with an extra shot of espresso, please." "Of course, Sheila."

Abby's face was a bright red. The shop had been full of life when we entered but the chatter had stopped and everyone sat or stood quietly while Abby worked. The gossip started again before the door closed when Sheila finally got her drink and we left.

"Is that what it's going to be like from now on, Whiskers? Is Roger finally going to get his way and ruin our new life on the beach?"

"Not if I can help it!" I meowed.

Sheila gave me a little scratch behind my ear before getting back in the golf cart and driving us to the Parrot Eyes Inn. We parked on the street and walked in the front door. Evelyn was already behind the reception desk. I hopped up onto my favorite chair beside the palm tree.

"I told you to go home and rest!"

Sheila wasn't going to listen this morning.

"I did. And now I'm back. If this really is your last day as an innkeeper, I'm not going to let you do it alone. We'll make sure everyone gets checked out then we can relax in the bar, finish off your supply of rum, and figure out how you're going to make the most of your retirement."

"I still haven't even buried ... "

Evelyn couldn't finish her sentence. She leaned over the reception desk holding her face in her hands. Sheila stepped forward and put her arm around Evelyn's shoulders. Neither of them moved or said anything for a couple of minutes until the elevator dinged. Evelyn quickly straightened up and tried to prepare herself to deal with a guest but Sheila ushered her into the office behind them.

"I've got this one. You take a minute."

Max stepped out of the elevator and walked toward Sheila.

"I've got the first session today. I'd just like to make sure the conference room will be cat-free this morning."

He glared at me and then looked expectantly at Sheila.

"I'll make sure Whiskers is otherwise occupied, Mr. Sharp. I hope you've enjoyed your stay." He smiled smugly.

"Indeed I have. A very successful visit."

Max glared at me again then walked toward the conference room, passing Victor Bloodworth who nodded curtly on his way to speak with Sheila. He was pulling a large suitcase across the carpet.

"Good morning, Mr. Bloodworth. Are you heading out already?"

"No, no. Can't skip the last two sessions. But I do have an appointment to make this afternoon so I'll need to leave promptly. I've vacated my room and would like to settle my bill now. Also, if you have somewhere you could hold my bag I would be forever grateful."

Evelyn had collected herself and came out of her office.

"I've got this, Sheila. There is no bill for you, Mr. Bloodworth. I'll be happy to keep your bag until you're ready for it."

Victor looked confused. "I'm certain that I accrued some incidental charges during my stay."

"It's been taken care of. And your room charge has been refunded. I can't expect you to pay for a room where your personal property was stolen by a hotel employee."

Victor stood silent for a moment, looking softly at Evelyn. Eventually, he nodded and smiled a gentle smile.

"My condolences on the loss of your son. I thank you for your generosity, although it is not necessary, and I assure you that when I speak of the

Parrot Eyes Inn I will do so with praise for both the establishment and its charming owner."

Victor set his bag beside the desk, tipped his fisherman's cap, and walked away.

I stared at Victor, thinking about his connection to Kevin's death. He seemed far too nice a man, and gentle, to have committed the crime. If he had done it then the man was an even better actor than author, standing there looking into the eyes of the victim's mother without showing any signs of guilt.

The clock was ticking, though, with the judge deciding on Roger's release on bail in less than two hours. If he got out, he could very well come after Sheila and the others to make sure there were no witnesses left to testify against him.

Conference attendees began filing through the lobby, some heading straight to the conference room and others visiting Sheila and Evelyn at the front desk, preparing to leave as soon as the sessions were finished. By nine o'clock they had all gone in to watch Max's presentation and the lobby was quiet.

Evelyn pulled a book and some paper from the desk drawer. "Did you leave these here last night?" she asked Sheila.

"Those papers need to be thrown away before Chief Anderson sees them. It's a printed-out email that we aren't supposed to have. The book is Tarrie Ann's. Sort of. She wants to get it signed but I can't imagine why. It's horrible."

"Sounds like my favorite kind of book! The worse the book is, the less I get nervous reading it." She set the papers down and opened the book to the middle, reading aloud in a melodramatic, sultry voice.

"You've ripped the sleeve of your uniform, Detective Hardbody. You need to slow down at the gym or you'll be buying a whole new wardrobe."

Evelyn changed voices to a deep and mysterious manly tone.

"Call me Todd. The gym is the only place I can forget about the bad things I've had to do. Very, very bad things."

Sheila laughed as she picked up the papers and carried them to the waste basket. Suddenly she stopped laughing, stared at the papers, and her jaw dropped.

"Evelyn, call the girls. We need them here. I'm calling Chief Anderson. I think I know who killed your son."

Nineteen

Half an hour later, Sheila, Evelyn, Tarrie Ann, Becky, and Julia were all huddled around the reception desk. Becky was dressed impeccably with her trademark stiletto heels and business suit. Tarrie Ann wore a simple dress and sandals. Julia had shown up in mismatched pajamas, a Christmas pattern on the full-length bottoms and tropical birds on the top.

The front door opened and Danny, the cameraman from News 5 Miami stepped in carrying his camera, a microphone, and a tripod. He used his right leg to hold the door open for Pamela Prince who held only a paper cup with the

Sea Brews logo like the one found at the crime scene. Julia gasped and hid behind the reception desk again.

"Who called them?" Sheila asked.

A deep voice with a Southern drawl answered. "I did, and you're welcome."

Chief Anderson stepped in behind the reporter.

"Ms. Prince is here to let the world know that the allegations of police misconduct are false. And that you ladies haven't been killing people so that you can investigate."

Sheila's frown was quickly replaced by a big grin. "So I was right?"

"Indeed, you were. All along, it seems, at least in some regards. Now, where will I find our killer?"

Sheila pointed to the closed door of the conference room.Pamela Prince waved her fingers at her cameramen, sending him to set up his camera while she looked at herself in a handheld mirror and adjusted her hair.

Danny rushed ahead and quietly made his way into the room. Chief Anderson walked over to where the ladies were gathered. I padded over and jumped onto the reception desk to listen.

"How did you know?" he asked Sheila.

"Detective Whiskers told me." She reached over and rubbed my badge with her sleeve like she was polishing it. I held my head high and purred loudly, proudly.

Chief Anderson just looked at us both skeptically. "Well, let's get this over with before the judge announces his decision. I'd hate for her to embarrass herself." He led the way as we all walked to the conference room and stepped inside.

Max stared at us from the lectern at the front of the large room. His left hand held the laser pointer which he quickly dropped as soon as noticed me walking beside Sheila.

"What's going on?"

Max's eyes grew wider as he seemed to notice Danny and his camera for the first time. I guess he'd been engrossed in his presentation and hadn't seen him slip in earlier.

Pamela moved in front of the camera, took the microphone from Danny, and spoke.

"We are live in Paradise Cove where the local police chief, with the help of the Paradise Cove Murder Society, has made a breakthrough in the murder that was committed here two nights ago. Chief Anderson will now reveal who the killer is on live television!"

The chief looked at her, stunned. He had invited her but hadn't realized she was planning a live reveal. Pamela pointed to the lectern and nodded her head, encouraging him to step up and tell the world what had been discovered.

Chief Anderson slowly walked to the front of the room and stood in front of the lectern as Max moved aside. The conference attendees looked around at each other, wondering what was happening.

"I, uh ... I have been working day and night to bring the killer to justice. This case has been puzzling from the start with all of the evidence pointing toward Roger Cabot, a man who was locked up in prison at the time of the murder. It has been suggested that the ladies of the Paradise Cove Murder Society fooled my police department in an attempt to frame Mr. Cabot. I can tell you now that, Mr. Cabot was, indeed, framed."

A loud murmur rose up from the writers. A few of them blurted out "I told you so." Max addressed Chief Anderson. "So what are you going to do to these women?"

"I'm going to thank them," the chief answered. "Ladies, please join me up here."

The murmurs grew louder. Tarrie Ann didn't hesitate. She strode forward immediately. Sheila and Becky followed sheepishly behind. Evelyn quietly took a seat at a back table. Julia, in her pajamas, stood as still as a statue directly behind Danny and his camera. Pamela walked over and nudged her forward and Julia reluctantly joined the others. I hadn't been invited but I padded up, as well, intentionally rubbing Buffy's ankle as I passed her. She sneezed. I jumped up on the rectangular table the ladies were standing behind and positioned myself where the camera would catch my freshly polished badge.

Max set his laser pointer on the table.

Chief Anderson continued.

"The ladies of the Paradise Cove Murder Society are not the ones who framed Roger Cabot."

A few people snickered. Buffy spoke up again.

"So, who did?"

"Mr. Cabot framed himself."

Gasps went up around the room.

"But he was not alone. Someone in this room assisted him."

The chief paused long enough to let his audience look around at each other accusingly then he looked at Victor Bloodworth.

"The list of possible suspects was limited to anyone who could have been in the pool area when the victim was struck by the umbrella and drowned in the pool. Most of you were in the bar together at the time of the murder so you were able to provide alibis for each other. Almost all of you told us that you saw Mr. Bloodworth leaving the bar shortly before the body was discovered."

All heads turned to stare in disbelief at the gentlemanly older man who kept a stone-faced expression.

"But we know where he was," Chief Anderson stated. "He was tending to a personal matter that does not need to be disclosed."

Victor nodded politely at the chief, looking relieved.

"Isabella Nightshade, you say that you were walking on the beach by yourself but we haven't been able to locate any witnesses who saw you. And we know that the victim overheard rumors about you stealing a story from another author to write your best-selling novel. He approached you with a USB drive stolen from Mr. Bloodworth and offered to sell it to you."

The crowd turned to look at Isabella and my sensitive cat ears picked up a few more "I told you sos."

"But the USB drive was still in the victim's possession when he was killed. We did not find any evidence that you had touched it."

Isabella glared around at the writers around her. Chief Anderson held up a USB drive.

"This is not the USB drive in question. That has been returned to its rightful owner. This USB drive has evidence that I was just sent minutes ago. May I?"

The chief looked at Max who reluctantly agreed to let him plug it into the computer controlling the display on the large projector screen. After a few moments, the image on the screen showed a video of Roger in prison clothes. He was sitting in a visiting area talking to someone whose back was to the camera.

"Mrs. Sheila Mason here," The chief pointed at Sheila, "suggested that I look at prison surveillance video from when a certain Todd Hardbody visited the prison. We believe that it was during this meeting that the final elements of a plan were put in place to frame Roger Cabot in order to cast doubt on the evidence in his trial for the previous murder."

The room fell silent until the visitor in the video stood up and turned around. One by one, people began to laugh and nudge whoever was beside them. Soon they all had realized that Todd Hardbody was Max, wearing a fake mustache and wig.

"You'll notice the visitor is carrying away a coffee cup with a Sea Brews logo on it. This is how Mr. Cabot's DNA ended up at the crime scene."

Max started to run toward the door but a loud growl stopped him in his tracks. Kojak and Officer Reid had stepped in quietly and were guarding the room's only exit. Max stood still with a resentful snarl.

Tarrie Ann held up the book with Max's name clearly showing in large, bold letters on the cover and read a line out loud.

"Detective Todd Hardbody picked up the perp and threw him across the room, his massive biceps ripping yet another shirt. A small price to pay for justice."

She looked at Max. "You haven't signed it for me yet. Do you mind? It's Tarrie with two r's and an ie. Ann without an e."

Laughter filled the room.

Chief Anderson let the laughter start to die down then cleared his throat to get everyone's attention again.

"I believe most of you were in the session when Mr. Sharp discussed his expertise in creating false IDs like the one we believe he used for his visit to the prison. I would appreciate your statements confirming that to be used in his trial."

Max spoke up. "It was during that session that the bloody gloves showed up on your desk, though, so how could I have put them there if I was leading the session?"

"I asked myself the same question. Then I remembered that it was during my interview with you, immediately after the session, when I discovered the gloves on the desk. As I recall now, you entered the office before I did, giving you just enough time to place the gloves and make it appear they had been there all along. I'm embarrassed to admit that it almost worked."

Pamela Prince interjected a question. "We reported earlier, Chief Anderson, that you had checked the gloves out of evidence. How did Mr. Sharp get them?"

"From a golfing supply store, I would imagine." Chief Anderson fiddled with the computer and a different video popped up on the projector screen. "This is the CCTV footage from when I supposedly signed out the evidence from the state facility. As you can see, the person in this video looks a lot more like Detective Hardb... Excuse me, Max Sharp. We believe that he purchased the gloves that Roger Cabot told him to purchase, waited until the evidence clerk was away from his desk, and signed the log with my name, indicating that he — or I — was taking the gloves even though they were still locked away. He even made sure to carry his new gloves as he left so that the video would show him with what appeared to be the evidence. The hope was that whoever checked the video wouldn't know what I looked like since I'm just a local cop in a small town."

"What about the fingerprints on the murder weapon?" Pamela Prince asked.

"Ah, yes. Thank you for reminding me. The umbrella used in the crime looked like all of the other umbrellas around the pool here at the hotel."

Chief Anderson paused and looked directly at me for a moment. He was clearly remembering the scene I had made that night, rubbing up against the umbrellas still in place at each of the tables. I held my breath, returning his gaze.

This was it. The moment I had been waiting for my entire career. The police chief was about to acknowledge my contributions to a big case. The badge on my collar felt heavy, pressing against my chest which was swelling up with pride. Out of the corner of my eye, I could see Kojak nodding his head with the beginnings of a smile. We cats don't cry like humans do but I could almost feel tears welling up in my eyes. I wished Fred could have been here to witness this moment.

Chief Anderson coughed and looked back toward the TV camera.

"Excuse me, sorry. Just running things through my head quickly. Where was I? Oh, yes. It occurred to me that, although we had an umbrella on the ground, no umbrellas were missing from the tables outside. As you know, the victim's mother owns this hotel and he had been conspiring with Mr. Cabot when the previous murder took place. Our theory is that Mr. Cabot had long ago been given one of the hotel umbrellas for his personal use at his home. His fingerprints were on it and he directed Mr. Sharp to where he would find it, neatly packaged in its plastic container which preserved the fingerprints. It was that umbrella, not one taken by chance from the pool area, that was used in the murder here two nights ago."

I couldn't believe it. Chief Anderson knew that I had solved the mystery but he refused to give me any credit. I turned to look at Kojak who just hung his head.

It was me who realized there was an extra umbrella. Kojak had noticed the coffee cup at the scene. Sheila connected the dots between the visitor log and the character in Max's book. But Chief Anderson stood there in front of all of the writers and the television audience and took the

credit. He had mentioned that Sheila told him to look at the prison surveillance video but that's as far as he would go in sharing the spotlight. I was disgusted.

But I was also relieved. A true detective doesn't do the job for glory. Fred had told me that many times when we solved cases together and watched his old boss doing all the interviews. The important thing was following the evidence and protecting the community, especially Sheila. We had done that. Instead of getting released from prison, Roger would have to prepare for two murder trials. Sheila's reputation was intact again. I couldn't wait to see everyone's faces the next time she stood in line for coffee at Sea Brews.

Officer Reid was handcuffing Max in front of the TV camera and all the conference attendees had gotten up from their seats. Sheila stepped over to the chief.

"What about the video of Roger outside the prison? Was that real? Kevin sure seemed to believe it."

"Fake. Kevin's phone finally dried up enough to turn on yesterday. We looked at the screenshot he was planning to show you and it had been doctored. I suspect that when we get a look at Max's phone we'll find the original video taken in the waiting area at the prison. He probably used some fancy software to replace the background. It's not hard to do these days."

"Roger did all this to make it look like you were incompetent and I was a crazy murderer just killing people for fun and games. And I bet he promised Max the exclusive rights to his story, which would have gotten tons of publicity. That must be the new book Max was so excited about."

"And they might have gotten away with it if it hadn't been... well... if we hadn't figured it out together. How did you know about Todd Hardbody?"

Sheila looked at me and grinned.

"I already told you. It was because of Detective Whiskers."

Chief Anderson looked down at me sitting on the table. I stood up on all four paws, poked my chest and my badge out, and turned around with my tail up high, showing him my one hairless spot as I padded away quietly.

TWENTY

The writers were all talking to each other excitedly or trying to get another interview with Pamela Prince. Sheila and I walked over to where Evelyn sat alone at one of the round tables.

"I'm so sorry, Evelyn. At least it's over now."

"Thank you, Sheila. For everything. I never could have gotten through this without you and your friends. And you, Whiskers!" Evelyn reached down and scratched my cheek. I rubbed up against her ankle.

"Are you going to close the inn?"

"I don't think I have any choice. Even with all of your help we barely made it this far. I just don't have the energy or the resources to get things back in shape again."

"Please pardon my interruption."

We all instantly recognized the pleasant English accent.

Evelyn stood up. "Mr. Bloodworth. You need your bag. I'll go get it for you."

"Please, call me Victor. And I'm in no rush. It seems the final session will be canceled so there's plenty of time to reach my appointment. I wondered if we might discuss another matter?"

Victor pulled out a chair for Sheila. After she and Evelyn were seated he eased himself into a chair. I hopped up onto the table, away from the careless footsteps of the people walking around.

"I'm certain that you don't recall, but I have been a guest in your wonderful inn before. Many years ago when you and your husband were running it together and providing your visitors with the very best personal service. I had always hoped to return and tried to stay aware of developments in this charming community. When I read about the exploits of the Paradise Cove Murder Society I insisted that our group meet here for this conference. I must apologize that my choice inadvertently led to your son's untimely demise."

Victor looked softly at Evelyn. There was a certain amount of pleading in his expression as if hoping for forgiveness.

Evelyn looked away from Victor for a moment. She was facing me and I could see the pain in her eyes. She took a deep breath and looked back at him.

"You have nothing to apologize for, Victor. Kevin made poor choices in life. His father and I tried to steer him back. We gave him every opportunity, but he never could straighten up. Even at the very end, he was trying to take advantage of you for profit. I still love him very much. I hope that doesn't offend you."

"To the contrary, it merely reinforces my very high opinion of you. And you have made some fine friends, I see."

Sheila blushed. Tarrie Ann, Becky, and Julia had spotted us. They walked over and each sat down. Victor tipped his fisherman's cap to each of them and continued speaking.

"I have one other confession to make. I abhor eavesdropping but I couldn't help hearing you say that the Parrot Eyes Inn would be closing forever. It is my hope that I might dissuade you from that decision."

Evelyn shook her head. "You've seen the condition this place is in. It's nothing like it was when you came here before. I've done all that I can and it's time for a new chapter."

"Ah, I love new chapters!" Victor smiled. "I have a proposal, if you will hear me out." He turned to Becky. "Based upon the description my associate gave me of a lovely lady in the tallest of heels, I believe that you may be the real estate agent I have been dealing with indirectly."

Becky's jaw dropped. "You're the buyer that's interested in the hotel."

"I am indeed."

Becky regained her composure and went straight into sales mode.

"I'm sure you've noticed that we've already been working on repairs. The opportunities here are ..."

Evelyn put her hand on Becky's arm and shook her head.

"He's been here for three days, Becky. He knows how much work is needed."

Victor smiled. "Indeed I do. But I have not forgotten the jewel it once was. I have only one concern."

We all waited. The hopeful smiles around the table had turned to worried looks.

"I believe that you ladies have deduced the reason for my occasional disappearances. It was kind of the chief to respect my privacy earlier, and I hope that you all will do the same. My appointment later today is with a neurologist who is overseeing the trial of a very promising new treatment for Parkinson's Disease. The medical records on my USB drive are for him. As hopeful

as I am that he will be able to help me, I, like Evelyn, have no intention of being responsible for the day-to-day operations of a hotel."

Everyone nodded their heads slowly. Chief Anderson and Officer Reid walked by, leading Max out. Victor stood up.

"Perhaps, Max, you have reconsidered my generous offer now that the prospects for your next book have dimmed and you find yourself in need of a good attorney?"

Max glared at Victor and then reluctantly asked Officer Reid to open his messenger bag. He reached in with his handcuffed hands and pulled out the book he had been carrying when he walked into the lobby smiling so widely the day before. He dropped it on the floor. Tarrie Ann held up the book she had taken from his room, along with a pen but he ignored her as he was led out the door. Julia picked the book off the floor and handed it to Victor.

"Thank you. Please forgive me that interruption. Where were we?"

Evelyn answered

"You were saying that you don't have time to run a hotel."

"Ah, yes. Thank you. So there would be one very important condition if I were to agree to pay the full asking price and invest the funding to restore the Parrot Eyes Inn to its former glory."

He looked at Sheila.

Sheila looked back, her eyebrows lowered in a question.

"I would require the services of a highly qualified and dedicated manager."

Sheila maintained her questioning look.

Victor maintained his patient gaze on Sheila.

"What? Do you mean me?" she finally asked.

Victor nodded.

"You said highly qualified. I've never managed a hotel."

"You did for the last three days, at full capacity and with a murder investigation going on all around you. I have no doubt that, with my funding and your careful attention, the Parrot Eyes Inn will once again be the most desirable vacation resort on the Gulf Coast."

Can't wait for the next Detective Whiskers adventure? The next book is Mission Impawsible.

Thank you for reading Purrder, She Wrote

I hope you're enjoying the adventures that Whiskers and Sheila are taking. Both of their lives have changed dramatically and they are meeting the changes head on. Ready for another adventure? Book five in the series is titled Mission Impawsible.

May I ask a favor of you? As an author, my number one goal is to have people read my stories. The more people the better, but I want my stories to reach the right readers. The people who will enjoy them and, hopefully, get something positive from them. That's why reviews mean so much to me. Every time you leave a review for one of my books it helps other readers know if the book has what they are looking for. The more you describe the story and characters (without giving out spoilers!) the more likely it is that someone searching for exactly this book will find it. If you don't like to leave reviews that's okay. I still appreciate you very much!

Have you signed up for my newsletter? I won't flood you with emails but I do make sure my newsletter readers are the first to know about new releases and special promos. Sometimes I'll do giveaways and special events that you only know about if you get the newsletter. You can sign up now at AuthorChrisAbernathy.com.

There's so much happening with social media that it's hard to keep up. I haven't been able to develop a meaningful presence on all of the platforms but I am active on Facebook. If you'd like to follow me there you can find me at facebook.com/authorchrisabernathy. It's a great way for us to interact with each other.

Okay, I'm going to get back to writing new stories for Sheila and Detective Whiskers. Keep reading to find out how to make Julia's spicy guacamole.

Each of the books in the Detective Whiskers Cozy Mystery Series is dedicated to a cat who has gone above and beyond the call of duty to protect and serve its loved ones. We don't know the name of the cat we are honoring in this book but we know that he helped the police in the most catlike way possible. By simply giving a suspicious look.

Police in Ephrata, Pennsylvania were trying to arrest 23-year-old Michael Steggy but he ran and hid when they showed up. The search was on and one police officer noticed a black cat staring intently in the direction of a shed. The officer searched the shed but found no sign of the fugitive. The cat, however, continued staring in the way that only a cat can. Eventually, the officer realized that the cat was staring past the shed he searched and at another shed further away. And that's where Steggy was found and arrested.

Good job, Mr. black cat, whoever you are!

Acknowledgments

There are a lot of people who have helped me to make these books come to life. In this book, I want to specifically acknowledge my mother, Carol Abernathy. My mom loved books more than anything else besides her family, friends, and cats. Her favorite day of the year was the preview day for the library book sale at the Anniston-Calhoun Public Library. Each year she donated some books but we always ended up with more than we started with. Our small church had an enviable church library, and still does, thanks in large part to her efforts to organize and build the collection. There is no doubt that my love for reading came from my parents and it is one of the best gifts they gave me.

RECIPE

Julia's Spicy Guacamole

Guacamole is a simple dish that anyone can make at home. What makes Julia's guacamole so special is the extra kick she gives it. It's the perfect appetizer to serve with any of Tarrie Ann's margaritas.

<u>Ingredients</u>

- Four large avocados
- One-quarter cup of minced white onion
- Four garlic cloves, minced
- One-half of a large jalapeno
- One full habanero
- One-third cup cilantro, chopped
- Juice from one lime

- One teaspoon of kosher salt

Directions

- Remove and discard the seeds from the peppers then chop them finely.
- Scoop the flesh of the avocados into a mixing bowl. Bonus points if you have a molcajete.
- Add the other ingredients except the cilantro to the bowl and mash together. Keep going until it's all mixed together but stop before you remove all of the texture. Some small lumps are essential to a great guacamole. Add most of the cilantro and gently fold it into the mixture. Taste and add more salt and/or lime juice until it tastes just right. Use the remaining cilantro as garnish.

Added tip

People say looks don't matter but we all know that they do, and this is especially true when it comes to food. You can serve just about any kind of chip (or several vegetables) to dip into the guacamole but if you go the extra mile and find some blue chips or something else in a color that pops against the green of the guacamole it will taste better, I promise.

Okay, that's the end of Purrder, She Wrote. Time for book five — Mission Impawsible!

Made in the USA
Middletown, DE
24 November 2023

43386161R00120